FOUR NIGHTS TO
THE FIREWORKS

Philip Purser

SAPERE
BOOKS

FOUR DAYS TO THE FIREWORKS

Published by Sapere Books.

24 Trafalgar Road, Ilkley, LS29 8HH

saperebooks.com

ISBN: 978-0-85495-505-3

For Ann

CHAPTER 1: TUESDAY

After three uneventful years James Dell was getting careless. He filled in the form quickly, name, address, date of birth, married or single, number of children, name of doctor and when last consulted, all in the flying, shapeless, ballpen capitals he used for job tickets and parts requisitions. The works manager was looking at him across an untidy desk and saying, 'I don't think you'll regret it, although you're a bit late to be joining a pensions scheme — what are you, thirty-seven?'

'Not quite.' The ballpoint squeaked as he jabbed a line through a section of the form that inquired about serious illness and scrawled his signature at the bottom.

'Especially now you're getting on in the firm,' said the works manager. 'You could be in a management job before you finished. It's possible. Then you'd wish you'd contributed all right. It'd be a difference of hundreds a year. You know that?' He took the completed form that Dell pushed across to him and studied it. Dell looked at the calendar on the wall behind the works manager's head. It came from the engineering group that supplied them with brake linings and it showed a girl kneeling by a fire and warming her hands. It wasn't clear what she had to do with brake linings. She wasn't wearing anything except a straw hat tilted back from her head.

'I thought you said not quite thirty-seven,' said the works manager. 'According to this you're half-way to thirty-eight.'

'What date did —?' asked Dell, trying too late to bite the question back.

'May. May the eighth.' He frowned. 'Don't remember?'

'I was all mixed up,' said Dell. 'Must have been thinking of the wife's birthday. I'll forget my own name next.' The works manager flicked the form back to him. 'You'd better change it. What's the right date?'

'October thirty-first.'

'You're a bright one! Do you know when October thirty-first it? It's *today*.'

'It's never,' said Dell lamely. He looked back at the calendar, this time at the panel of dates below the picture.

'You can take my word for it.' He stared at Dell. 'You're a bright one, forgetting your own birthday.'

'I was thinking it was tomorrow. I was sure it was a Wednesday. We were going to —'

'Yes, well that's all right. Another few years and you'll wish you could forget all about birthdays.'

Dell was still scowling at his mistake as he scrubbed his hands ten minutes before knocking-off time. He muttered, *Stupid bugger* at the thin, guarded face reflected in the mirror above the wash basin.

'What's that?' said the man at the next basin.

'Nothing. Forgot something, that's all.' He concentrated on his hands, scooping some more gritty red cleaning compound and working away at the dirt-engrained lines that criss-crossed the right index finger and thumb. They were garage hands, all right. They reassured him as he rinsed them under the warm trickle from the tap. All the same, on the way home he doodled on the strip of his ticket. Must remember things like birthdays, October 31st, October 31st, October 31st, not any other. He rolled the paper into a tight ball and dropped it in the Used Ticket Box as he got off.

Dell took two buses home, the first along the arterial road as the high yellow lights came on in the dusk; the second winding away through beech woods and patches of river mist. It was an awkward journey, often broken by a long wait but it suited Dell's purpose. No one else from the works lived in the same area; no one even took the same second bus. He could keep work and home apart. It was good security. On the back of the second ticket he worked out some matters of small finance. Tuesday: three full journeys still to come, at 1s. 8d. a time; two canteen dinners at four bob. The figures ran into each other as the bus lurched. He leaned back in his seat, inspecting the anonymous, switched-off faces of the other passengers. A girl in a fuzzy wool coat stared blankly across the aisle; a fat man had his eyes closed, his heavy chops trembling with the vibration of the motor.

At the church stop Dell nodded to the West Indian conductor and turned up the steep lane to the Common. It was a longish climb. Dell enjoyed it, whistling until the steepness made him short of breath. The iron segments on his heels rang on the road. At the top of the hill the sound was abruptly stilled as he transferred to the softness of the bridle path. He stopped and listened for a moment, then went on. Wire netting separated the path from a scrubby grey wood. In the gloom a flashlight hovered over a row of hutches. Dell sniffed, spat, and yelled ritually, 'Stinking things.'

Ahead were the subdued lights of the cottage. Dell started to unbutton his mac. The door opened straight into the living room. Dell fumbled through the blanket hung behind it and was immersed in the paraffin-heavy cosiness within. The tin bath was in the middle of the floor, a pink, celluloid duck floating still in the water. Nancy sat on the cane chair drying the baby. The baby wriggled and grinned, showing two outsize square teeth, and said, 'Da-da.'

Dell made a gruff pecking noise. The baby was convulsed with delight. Her legs kicked excitedly under the towel. Dell said, 'You're early with her tonight.'

'I thought I'd try and be. It's your birthday. I forgot.'

'I did myself. I was with Wright. It could have been awkward.'

'What are you? Thirty-seven?'

'That or only seven. It would depend which way you looked at it.'

'Thirty-seven the way I look. Tony's upstairs. I kept him in bed again. You know how he gets when he's had a cold.'

'I'll go up and have a word with him.' He took off his mac and muffler and hung them on the hook at the side of the dresser. 'Those minks don't half stink. The wind must be the wrong way.'

'Do you want a cup?'

'No. I'll wait.' He bent his head and clumped up the stairs. Tony's door was open and he was sitting up in his camp bed expectantly.

'Mum brought some fireworks for Guy Fawkes,' he said. The fireworks were in a cardboard box on the bed.

'Oh,' said Dell. 'She did, did she?' He glanced up at the paraffin lamp on top of the cupboard, measuring the distance of the flame. He moved a plate and mug from the chair by the bed and sat down. 'Let's have a look.' Holding the little blue-spotted one that said 'Golden Rain', hearing the filling shake inside, brought back a momentary sensation of childhood. There was a hard, thin red one, too, that was still called 'Little Wizard'.

'That's a banger,' said Tony, clapping his hands to his ears in demonstration.

'Let's put 'em away now, eh?' He closed the box and put it on the floor. 'What else did you do today?'

'Looked at my books and played with my cars and Mum came up with the wireless once.' The bed was littered with confirmatory evidence: half-a-dozen Dinky cars, a bigger friction-drive model, catalogues and old motoring magazines that Dell had brought home from the works.

'Did you make any pictures?'

'Yes. I made two. No, four.' He hunted around in the junk that had accumulated on the bed. 'I did this one last.'

Dell took it. Tony's little old man's face was lined with concentration, willing him to approve. The picture showed the cottage. It was done in crayons and it wasn't bad for six. Tony could draw if he couldn't do much else. Dell frowned at an item in the foreground, square with wheels and a man's face visible through the windscreen. He said, 'You put the doctor in. Was he here today then?'

'Not the doctor. Another car.'

Dell said, 'You don't get cars along here, except the doctor's; and he'll get stuck again if he comes when it's muddy. You only get cars on the proper roads.'

'There was a car today. I sore it.'

'Where? When?'

'Out the window. I was sitting up to dror.'

'You sure? Not making it up?'

'No. I sore it. It stopped outside and the man got out and walked around. Then he went in again.'

'Where was Mum? Did she see him?' He managed to keep the urgency out of his voice.

'No. I think she was at the shops.'

'Did you tell her when she came back?'

'Yes, I said her when she came up.' Concentration exaggerated the chevron lines of worry on Tony's face, made him look even older. He started to wheeze.

Dell stood up. 'That's all right, Tone. I'll come up and see you again before bed.'

The baby was in the old highchair now, dressed in old pyjamas that had been Tony's before. The top half didn't match the bottom and both looked grey to Dell. Nancy was ladling pink blancmange into the comical little mouth. The baby beamed at Dell and a bit slopped out.

'What's all this about a car being here?'

'Oh, something that Tony made up. He's crazy about cars ever since you brought him those papers.'

'He says it's true.'

She shrugged, more concerned to get the baby fed.

'Why d'you want to give her that stuff?' said Dell absently. 'Isn't she a bit young to be having that stuff? And another thing: what are those fireworks doing on Tony's bed?'

'Now just a minute!' She flashed him a quick bright look of battle. 'Have you anything else while you're in the mood? Or is that the lot?'

'I'm only trying to point out that fireworks are explosive and that Tony's got them littered all over his bed with a paraffin lamp about five feet away. Anyway, what does he want with fireworks? He was frightened out of his skin the only time he heard any.'

'Listen, that's just why I got him them. If you want him scared like a rabbit all his life I don't. Anyway he asked me for some. He saw the bonfire they're building along at Price's farm. And they didn't come out of the housekeeping if that's what you're worrying about.'

'Well I'll get them down after and put them in a safe place,' said Dell. He wasn't in a mood for fighting. 'Where's the torch?'

'Where it always is.'

Dell found it on the dresser, propping up the Pools envelope. He wound on his muffler again and pushed his way through the blanket and out the door. The ground was firm but not iron hard; if there hadn't been much rain lately nor had there yet been a real frost. Dell switched on the torch and began to examine the bridlepath immediately outside the cottage. He found what he was looking for in a patch of softer earth where the path was worn wider for the turn in to the old shed: fresh tyre-marks. He shivered and went in again.

'There was a car,' he told Nancy. 'He wasn't making it up.'

'Maybe it was the doctor.' She'd finished feeding the baby and was fussing her up before bed, crooning and kissing the little round head.

'It wasn't the doctor. For one thing he said it wasn't the doctor and for another thing he drew a picture and it wasn't the doctor's car. Looked more like a two-seater hard top, an Alpine or something like that.'

'You'd go by Tony's drawing? And him only six!'

'He's all right at drawing. Especially cars. He's got a good eye for the line. Who do you think it could have been?'

'I don't *know*. Does it matter?' She swept the baby up to her shoulder bent to scoop an armful of bits of clothing and blankets.

'It matters a lot, I should have thought.' The baby looked at him over her mother's shoulder and beamed. Dell absently made a kiss-kiss noise.

'All right, I'll be down again in a minute.' She started up the stairs. 'This one must have some new pyjamas, poor little scrap.' She was talking to herself more than to Dell. When she came down she collected up a soggy nappy from the floor, took it out to the pail in the kitchen, came back, hunted on the mantelpiece for her cigarettes, lit one with a twist of paper from the fire.

Dell waited. From above came the thumping sound as the baby bounced her bottom in the cot. In a minute she'd probably cry before going to sleep.

Nancy rested momentarily on the arm of the old sofa and exhaled cigarette smoke gratefully. 'Phew! If I had a half-crown for every time I've been up those stairs today we'd be rich.' She looked at Dell. 'About the car: I was thinking. Couldn't it have been someone looking for the mink farm: I mean they could see the hutches from the road and think that was the turning. Then the fellow'd see he wasn't getting anywhere and stop here to ask the way…'

'Could have been, I suppose. But it never happened before, did it? Not in three years has anyone been here for the mink farm.'

'There's always a first time.'

Dell said, 'It's not the only thing. Last night I had a feeling someone was following me up the hill. I didn't think anything more of it but now … then there was something at the works a couple of weeks ago. I didn't tell you at the time. I was over at the stores chasing up some part or another and there was this man waiting at the same counter. He was a customer, not just one of the boys from the garages. He gave a sort of start when he saw me and smiled as if he were going to say hello. I pretended to be puzzling over the dockets I had in my hand. Luckily they brought him whatever he'd been waiting for but I could feel him staring at me while they made out the invoice.'

'You're stewing again. Honestly, it's nothing, a thing like that—'

'I haven't finished. He turned to go and said, "Haven't we met somewhere?" I said I didn't think so, in a sort of mumble, you know, and he shrugged and said he was sorry and went off.'

'There you are.'

'Just a minute. The point is, I remembered *him*.'

'What?'

'Well, I don't remember his name but I remembered his face. He was at King's, in the old life.'

'I wouldn't know about that,' said Nancy shortly. 'You don't tell me much about yourself then.'

'No point, it's best forgotten.'

'But I'd like to know. I'd like to know all about you, what sort of a kid you were, what you did at school, all that. All I'm allowed to share with you is the seven years since we met. It's like being married to a second-hand husband.'

Dell kicked at the logs in the fire. 'I'm worried enough without all that again. That wretched birthday, I only changed it because it's the kind of thing that could give you away if someone happened to notice it was the same as…'

'Look, love, nothing's happened, nothing's changed. You're imagining it. You saw someone who might have known you once, you heard your own footsteps on the hill, you forgot your birthday like anyone might —'

'I didn't only forget it. I gave the wrong one, the old one. And now there's this man in a car.'

'It's still nothing. Your trouble was all over and done with a long time ago. No one cares about what happened seven years ago. I didn't even know about it at the time.'

'It wasn't the kind of thing you'd find in Peg's Paper.' But he gave her a smile.

'Peg's Paper? Where did you dig that one up from?' She stood up again, pinching out her cigarette. 'Listen, it's your birthday. I've got something nice for your tea and afterwards let's go along to the pub for a drink.'

'What about the kids?'

'Oh, they'll be all right for half an hour. Just for once. It must be six months since I've been anywhere.'

'Well, I dunno about money,' said Dell doubtfully. 'I was hoping to save an extra quid this week…'

'That's all right. I've a few bob put by. Is it settled then?'

'If you like.' He added, 'It would be nice. Thank you.'

'Good. I'll get on now.' She ran her hand through his wiry hair as she passed. 'Don't worry. It's nothing, you'll see.'

Upstairs the baby cried, despairing bleats that died away to moments of silence, then came again. Dell looked round the cluttered little room. The sofa was broken at one end, the carpet had faded to an indeterminate brown, there was a damp patch on one wall and dark stains on the ceiling from the oil lamps. A pile of washed but unironed clothing occupied the one new easy chair; underneath it, a blue plastic pot. From the kitchen came sudden music as Nancy switched on the portable radio. Upstairs the crying stopped.

The Harrow had two tables and a dozen fairy lights outside in summer to try and catch the motorists. In winter it reverted to the custom of two or three dozen regulars. Dell hung back at the door.

'What's a matter?' said Nancy.

'You go first.'

'All right. Here, take this.'

Dell felt a note being pushed into his hand. He held the door open and looked past Nancy to see who was behind the bar. It was Cobb's wife. Cobb was the publican. He followed Nancy in and said, 'What would you like?'

'I'll have one of those cherry things.'

Dell went up to the bar and ordered it and a pint of Guinness and bitter for himself. Cobb's wife poured a little bottle of sticky red fluid into a conical glass with a bunch of purple cherries painted on the side. He carried it carefully over to Nancy. She was looking at the dirty postcards stuck on the wall, still there from summer. All the regulars sent one from wherever they went on holiday.

'Hey, look at this one,' said Nancy. 'It's a scream!'

There was a doctor with his stethoscope examining a busty girl. 'Big breaths,' he was saying. And she: 'Yeth, and I'm only thixteen.'

'It was on the wireless,' said Dell. 'Or in a film. And anyway, it's not all that funny.'

'Sorry, I'm sure.' She turned her back on the cards and sat down at a table.

'All right, I didn't mean it like that. Only you weren't really laughing, you were just putting it on and it sounded — well, you know, it sounded put on, and strained, and false.'

'I said I was sorry.'

Dell fetched his own drink, dark and creamy-topped in a tall glass. He said, putting it down on the table. 'No, it's me that's sorry. I shouldn't have said anything. It's just that I'm a bit unsettled tonight.'

She smiled a smile she had, of sudden total capitulation. 'Oh, go on with you. You were quite right.' She sipped her drink. 'It's your birthday. Cheers.'

'Cheers,' said Dell. He took a deep dive into the Guinness and bitter.

'You're funny about going in pubs. Why didn't you want to be first in here? I could tell you were all bristly. What is it?'

'I'm shy.'

She made a sound of disbelief.

'It's true. I don't want to get drawn into talking to strangers. You know why. And Cobb here, the landlord, I'm scared of him. Honestly.' He looked down into the creamy foam of his drink. 'I mean, he knows we live not far away but I don't come in for months on end. He probably thinks I go to some other pub…'

'And you care what he thinks, that great fat nobody?' She was wide-eyed with indignation.

'It's silly but I do. I can't help it.' He watched a windjammer ploughing endlessly through bright blue waves on some sort of trick revolving lampshade behind the bar. Mrs. Cobb was polishing a glass. A silver charm tinkled rhythmically on her wrist. 'Tell me about the baby. What did she do today?'

'She's a little duck. I sat her on the pot for the first time. She wasn't half surprised. Didn't do anything, of course. She's so fat her bottom stuck over the sides.'

'Did you take her to the doctor's for her inoculation?'

'How could I, with Tony in bed again?'

'You leave him to go shopping.'

'That's different. He wouldn't want to have been left after dark. Anyway, I thought the doctor might have come today to see him. He could have done the baby at the same time.'

'Did you ask him to come?'

'No, but…' She let the sentence die.

Dell said, 'I don't want it to be like the other jabs, dragging on for weeks after they should have been finished.'

'She means a lot to you, doesn't she?'

'Of course.'

'Like Tony doesn't?' She was back on the defensive.

Dell took her hand. It was work roughened but soft, and small by comparison with his own. The nails were nice, cut short and still pink and alive. 'Look, we don't need to go over all that again. Tony's all right. He's more to me than anyone, just as he is to you. Only it's different, because he's what he is. It's more a protective thing.'

'I know. When I see people looking at him because he's funny I want to — wrap round him, shield him, you know? I just feel it all welling up inside me. It's all right round here now. They know him.'

'Yes, but is he getting any better? They said that being higher up would help and here he is in bed again, and it's only October still.'

'Sometimes he seems a lot better, then he goes and gets another of his bad ones. I don't know what to think.' Her hand tightened in Dell's. 'Anyway, if what they say is true about him being born like that I don't see what difference it makes where we live.'

'Maybe somewhere hot is what he needs.' He hadn't been listening very hard to her. 'Lots of sun.'

'A fat chance of that.'

'If I hadn't done what I did it would be easy. I could have had a job any day in — in California or Nevada.'

'And if you hadn't done what you did you would never have met me. You wouldn't be living here. You wouldn't have had Tony. You'd have married some girl who went to college and you'd've had a proper, paid-up kid like anyone else.'

Dell shrugged. 'I suppose so. I'll get you another shot of that jungle juice.'

19

'No thanks. I've still got plenty.'

'I don't know how you can drink the stuff.'

'I knew you'd say that sooner or later. I like the taste. Do you mind?'

'I'm sorry. There I go again trying to take you over or something.'

'That's all right. I'm used to it. What you can get me is some fags.' She hunted in her bag. She was sitting as she always sat at a table, very straight. In the electric lights of the pub her hair looked fairer than it did at home but drier, too. There was the jingle of keys and money.

Dell swivelled round to see at the bar. 'Cobb's there now,' he whispered.

'So what?' She pushed a half-crown across the table. 'Ten Woods, and a box of matches.'

'I've still got plenty from what you gave me before.' He heaved up from the table and carried his empty glass over to the bar.

'Hullo there!' said Cobb. 'Did your friend find you? The one that was looking for you?'

They hurried back along the top road. It was very dark, a night of thick low cloud that hid the stars and moon. Once or twice a car swept by, the glare of its headlights softened by the hint of mistiness in the air. Nancy said, 'I don't see that rushing home'll make any difference. He'll find you there as easily as in the pub. Easier, in fact.'

'I don't intend to be found. We won't answer the door.'

'What good'll that do? He'll only come back tomorrow.'

'Then we'll put the lights out and lock up. He'll think no one lives there any more.'

'Some hope. Anyway, I bet you it's only someone from down the village. Or one of the test drivers from the works. They pass this way.'

'I don't know any of the test drivers.' He slowed suddenly. 'Unless it was the new one, Roberts or Richards or whatever his name is. I believe I did tell him I lived this way. He said he was looking for somewhere to live in the country himself.'

'There you are. I bet it was him.'

'But the car Tony saw wasn't one of ours. He'd have known from the pictures he's seen.'

'Look, he's only six. I'm twenty-five and I couldn't tell one car from another.'

'We ought to be getting back to them, anyway,' said Dell defensively.

As they neared the bridle path Dell steered Nancy to the soft verge of the road. The clatter of their footsteps was absorbed. 'I'll get my feet wet,' she whispered accusingly. At the turning in Dell held her still and peered through the darkness to the distant light of the cottage. 'Come on,' she said. 'There's nothing there. My feet are soaking.'

'Sssh.'

'It's all right for you. I need some new shoes. These have had it.'

They started, along the bridle path towards home. Dell was on the lookout for the glint of metal or glass that might come from a car parked near the cottage. It seemed all clear. Nancy took his arm in the dark. They passed the mink farm. Nancy withdrew her arm and hunted in her bag for the keys. Dell relaxed for the moment, and it was already too late when he saw a movement from the corner of his eye. The car had been backed right into the gateway to the shed, just beyond the cottage and screened from view by a tangle of holly.

'Mr. Dell,' said a voice. 'Mr. Dell!'

Nancy had the front door open, the curtain in her hand. The yellow light streamed out on to her. She slipped inside and reached the latch ready to bang it shut again. Dell shook his head. It wouldn't do any good. 'What do you want?' he said, roughening his voice.

The man was out of the car now, letting the door slam behind him. He said, 'I'm sorry if I startled you. I didn't see you coming, I must have been dozing.'

'What's the idea. Who are you?'

'If I could come in for a minute I'll explain.'

'I said what's the idea? Hiding like that?'

'I didn't want to miss you, that's all. I guessed you wouldn't be long.'

Dell grunted and stepped inside. The stranger followed. He'd unbuttoned a black city overcoat and was fumbling in an inner pocket. After a moment he said, 'I thought I might have a card.' He went on searching vaguely through his pockets. 'Anyway, my name's Hunter and I'm from the Sunday Press and I wondered if I could have a word with you...'

'If it's only a minute,' said Dell. He gave Nancy a quick despairing look.

Hunter gazed round him. He was shorter than Dell but he kept his shoulders bent as if afraid of catching his head on the low beams. He said, 'What a nice old cottage. And no electricity? You wouldn't think it was only thirty miles from London.'

Nancy said, 'Won't you sit down?' She started clearing baby clothes and the paper and teddy bear from the old sofa, bundling it all together in her arms. 'I'm afraid we're in rather a mess. We just slipped out for a minute, you know...' The 'know' was prolonged exaggeratedly. She'd put on her posh voice.

Hunter was fumbling in his pockets again. At the third try he produced a twenty-packet of Players. 'Do you smoke, Mrs. Dell?' Nancy took one. Dell shook his head. Hunter said, 'You don't mind if we do…?' Nancy struck a match and held it out, without taking her eyes off him. Dell waited. He could hear the uncertain rhythm of Tony's breathing upstairs. The damp patch by the door looked worse. Hunter took the plunge.

'On the paper,' he said, 'we're planning a series about Where are They Now? — about people who were in the news one time or another and have never been heard of since. You know the sort of thing.'

'I don't. I don't read that kind of paper.'

'Yes, well, lots of people say that. Actually it's not so bad, you know. Sometimes it's on the right side. Anyway, I'm supposed to work on this Where are They Now? So far we've got a couple of murderers and old Isaacs from the Shirreffs Tribunal — the battledress king — and an unfrocked priest, and the pilot of the airliner that killed all those people near Dagenham. Oh, and what's his name who ran away to Scotland with the oil heiress. And on the nicer side, there's an actress who gave up the West End to go and teach handicapped children, but they're not sure if they'll use her yet.' He paused and looked at the end of his cigarette, and then at Dell and then at Nancy. He had a sad face with an upper lip that folded over the lower.

Dell said, 'Put the kettle on, would you. I could do with a cup.'

'All right.' She went into the kitchen, shutting the door behind her to hide the unwashed tea things. A moment later the portable was switched on, tactfully loud, a snatch of music giving way to an announcer's voice.

Dell said, 'And what's all this got to do with us?'

Hunter looked uncomfortable. 'I was hoping I wouldn't need to tell you that...' As if reproaching himself for ineffectuality, he drew himself forward into a more businesslike posture and began again. 'Not to beat about the bush, Mr. Dell, we believe that you were — you were once known as Bristow, John Bristow, and that you were a scientist, that you ... umm ... were involved in the Cliente spy business but managed to disappear. To Russia, everyone thought. To the East anyway.' He stopped. His voice had tailed off from the brisk confidence with which he began.

Dell let a puzzled frown deepen on his face. 'I don't know what you're talking about. You must have got the wrong man.' He heard a burst of applause from the wireless and a loud officer-type voice trying to assert something over the top of it.

Hunter said, 'We have our reasons, you know. I mean, we don't just go and knock people up on the off-chance.'

Dell tried a laugh. 'Well, this time someone's been having you on. I'm in a garage at sixteen pounds a week plus a bit of overtime. We don't assemble atom bombs, either.'

'Yes, well, we know all about that.' He was at his pockets once more. 'Just a minute.' He started sorting through a wad of envelopes and bits of folded khaki paper. 'In fact you assemble imported cars. Nice, aren't they? Here we are. You've been there since September 1958 and you're now a supervisor? They think well of you. The prospects could be very nice indeed ... but before that you were in a garage in the Midlands, and before that in a bus depot in Liverpool. Started as a cleaner along with the Irish and the West Indians.'

'What are you driving at?'

'What were you doing *before* that, before '55?'

'I don't see what that's got to do with you.' Dell tried to counterfeit some anger.

Hunter sighed. 'I don't like this kind of job. I'm supposed to be a feature writer, not a toe in the door merchant. I don't want to go nosing into people's private life. But the office have got all the evidence anyway. I didn't put them on to it. They had it.'

'What evidence?' There was a burst of laughter from the wireless and another muffled voice trying to rise above it.

'Well, there's a physical description to start with, which fits except for the beard and of course that would have been the first thing Bristow would have done, shave it off. There's the fact that Bristow's never turned up anywhere, this side of the Curtain or the other. Sooner or later, you hear something about most people who go over. And for what it's worth there's the fact that the Russians have consistently denied knowing anything about him.' He shuffled through his bits of paper. 'That's all a bit negative, I admit. We come to some more positive items. You were married in Birkenhead in April '55 on papers that said you were a citizen of the Irish Republic. You'd used the same ones to get a National Health card four months earlier. In fact the man called Dell the papers referred to had gone to America, where he's now an engineer in Scranton, Philadelphia. He says he doesn't remember what happened exactly. He'd been working all summer as a site engineer. He went back to Trinity to take his finals in October and then went straight to America. He was in a house in Dublin with about six or eight other students. He presumes he left his insurance card and everything there. He says people tended to come and go in the house. He doesn't think there was anyone called Bristow.' He paused to throw his cigarette into the fire. 'We're not usually as thorough as this. You have to thank an eager beaver who's just joined the paper. They gave him the tip to work on.'

'Tip?'

'There's always a tip. Newspapers don't find much out for themselves. Now, handwriting: there's an accident report you had to write at the bus depot. They still had it on file. There is also a bunch of letters Bristow sent after his disappearance to his fiancée, Stella Rayner, posted at London Airport over a space of a few weeks. We've shown the letters and a photostat of the report to a tame handwriting expert and he says there's no doubt the same man wrote them. Incidentally, he said the letters were all written at the same time. Finally, local talk: they say you keep mainly to yourselves, not very sociable. People are sorry about your boy — asthma or something, is it? But Mrs. Dell has been known to hint in the shops that you've come down in the world.'

There was silence. In the kitchen came the clink of crockery and the wireless voice, suddenly clearer. Dell found himself listening, somehow, despite the situation. 'And now a question from the lady in the green hat there… Does the team think that with the Xmas cards already in the shops in October that Christmas is getting out of hand …'

Hunter said, 'Look, there's no point in beating about the bush. The story would be difficult to run without your cooperation, but it wouldn't be impossible — not for the kind of people on my paper. But it'd be much better with your cooperation, and there would be something in it for you. To be exact, we'd pay you say £200. A hundred now and a hundred on publication. I can't actually promise anything myself, but I should think that names and places could be disguised. As long as we have some pictures.'

Dell said, 'I don't know what you're talking about.' The words sounded loud and unreal.

An agricultural voice was in possession of the radio programme: 'I can only say what Oi've done the last two Christmasses and that's tell my grandchildren to wait until they see the whoites of Santa's eyes.'

Hunter stood up. 'Look,' he said. 'It's all a bit sudden. You need time to think it over. I'll get shot if they find out, but I'll pretend I didn't get you today, and I'll come back tomorrow. How's that? Would the same time be all right?'

'It won't do you any good,' said Dell. 'But come if you must.'

Hunter called, 'Good night, Mrs. Dell.' The wireless was turned down. Nancy's head appeared at the kitchen door. 'Oh, you're not stopping for a cup then?'

'Thanks, but I really have to be on my way. Perhaps I'll see you tomorrow.' His sad face was lit momentarily by a smile.

Dell stood at the door as the car engine caught first time. He watched the red tail lights lurching up the bridle path.

Nancy said behind him, 'What does it mean? What is it?'

Dell closed the back door behind him and warily trod the ten paces to the outside privy. Sometimes at night he didn't bother with it in the dark but stood against a tree instead, or a corner of the shed. Tonight he even shut the door behind him and listened to the water drumming into the earth five feet below. Outside again he shivered in the cold air. There was a wind getting up and the night seemed a little clearer than it had been. He picked his way carefully past the old well-head towards the shed. There were rickety double doors at the end that faced the path and a single door in the side facing the cottage. He had to lift it before he could drag it open. He stopped and struck a match to find what he was looking for in the litter inside. As the flame started to reach his fingers he located it behind a sack of cement solidified from damp and age. Without bothering to heave the door shut again he hastened back to the kitchen.

The old deed box was rusty where the japanning had worn; there was earth still under the hinges and handle, as if it had been buried. It was closed with an iron padlock, also rusty. Dell looked at it, perplexed, for a moment.

Then he hunted amongst the clutter of things on the dresser until he found a bunch of keys. There must have been twenty of them, from a massive iron door key to an old yellow Yale worn smooth as a Victorian penny. At third attempt he found the right squat key that sprung the padlock. The smell of damp papers rose as he opened the lid; there was a whisper as dust fell on to the kitchen table. Dell peered inside and lifted out a passport. Something had stained the cover, or rather bleached it, a pear-shaped mark that ran off the lower edge. The pages clung together lifelessly and the ink on the Description bit had started to run. The faded exhortation began, 'We, Ernest Bevin.' The date of issue was May 12, 1949, with a renewal stamped in five years later. Dell dropped it back into the box and shut the lid. It had finally expired in 1959.

In the middle of the night he lay restless and unsleeping. Curiously, he had fallen off soon after getting into bed, but Tony crying out in his sleep had woken him again. The old bed dipped in the middle, so that every wriggle tended to push him against Nancy. She would sometimes grunt and resist without waking. Dell lay on his side and stared at the light under the door from the lamp left burning on the landing and waited for sleep.

CHAPTER 2: WEDNESDAY

The alarm clock jangled, shrilly at first then deepening and slowing as the spring wound down. Nancy pushed an arm out in the cold air so she wouldn't fall asleep again. Her eyes were still closed. Dell mumbled, 'I hardly slept at all. I'll never get through the day. It would have been bad enough at any time. With what happened last night I just don't know.'

'You'd been laying there stewing again. You'll be all right.' She pushed the other arm out. 'What you going to do about it?'

'I don't know yet.' The room was still quite dark. The first greyness of dawn outside scarcely penetrated the little low window and its faded brown curtain.

Nancy sat up and slewed sideways from the bed in one movement. There was a flash of white body as her nightdress rode up. Then she was inside her dressing-gown and her slippers were on her feet. Dell listened to her slip slopping down the stairs. In a minute he'd have to force himself up too. From the cot at the foot of the bed came an exhalation and the beginnings of a cry; the baby was waking. She always slept through the alarm clock and woke five minutes later. Dell drew breath as if going to dive into icy water. The air was cold and a bit stale. Nancy was against opening the window at night. With a shiver he pushed himself up.

He pulled on underclothes, his work trousers, an old thick pullover. Downstairs two oil lamps were lit already. Dell raked the ashes of the fire through the firebars and went out to fetch the ash bucket and shovel, carrying the empty coal scuttle with him. In the kitchen a kettle and a saucepan were on the Calor stove and Nancy, stripped bare, stood on the brick floor washing herself all over at the sink. Sometimes Dell would slap her bottom and say, 'You must be crazy, you'll freeze to the floor.' Today he said nothing and went mechanically through the routine of clearing out the fireplace. By the time he'd finished and brought in the coal scuttle again she was dressed, though her hair was still in a tangle.

It was Dell's turn at the sink now. He shaved in hot water from the kettle, swilled his face and forearms, rinsed the little plate that held one front and one eye tooth and fumbled it into his mouth. He thought of something and broke the silence. 'Whatever else you do, don't forget the baby's inoculation.'

'I haven't forgotten.'

'You've said that before, and it still hasn't made any difference.' There was silence. 'And another thing: you'd better pick up the family allowances today.'

'Don't worry. I'm not likely to forget. You try feeding four on six pound a week.'

Dell buttoned up his shirt. 'Have you checked the getaway bags lately? Everything packed in them?'

'What?' She was startled. 'You're not thinking of moving on just because of that reporter man last night?'

'I don't know yet.' Dell knotted his tie. 'If we did' — his voice was muffled as he pulled on a grey pullover — 'it might only have to be temporary. You could start putting it about today that your mother's ill and you might have to go and stay with her.'

'I couldn't do that. Supposing she did get ill, really. I'd blame myself for wishing it on her.'

Dell bent down to comb his short, stiff hair with the aid of a triangle of broken mirror propped on the sill behind the sink. He said, 'This is not the time for superstitions, even new ones you've just made up. Your mum's ill and you're very worried about her. All right?'

Nancy finished laying the table in silence. Upstairs the baby was in full protest. Dell shook cornflakes into a bowl and soaked them in milk. He looked at the slices of bread on the table and said, 'Toast, why can't we ever have toast?'

Stephen, one of the mechanics, called. 'There's a fellow outside asking for you, in an ole black six.' He spelled out a registration number.

'Won't anyone else do?' said Dell. 'I'm busy.'

'Don't worry about me,' said the customer he was talking to. He had a bedraggled ginger moustache he'd been fidgeting with nervously. He was worried by his car, a little red van converted into a station wagon that stood jacked up between them.

'Well, if you're sure you don't mind. I'll only be a moment.'

'That's all right. I need time to think.'

Dell walked through the big sliding doors of the service shop to the back area. It was corrugated iron and asbestos panels here, the glass façades and neon signs and beds of tulips were presented only to the main road through the estate. A close parked huddle of cars awaiting attention overflowed into the verge of the cinder road leading to the next factory. The dull black saloon Stephen had identified was at the very end of the line; the driver was by its side; he had a rear door open and was looking for something inside the car. Dell was still five yards away when the lens or the man's attitude or whatever it was suddenly registered. There was a flood of bright light. He stopped dead and looked behind him in panic. No one seemed to be watching. He turned again, ducking his head behind his arm and said, 'What the hell's the idea. Who are you?' Even as he spoke the man swung the camera up in a quick, very controlled motion and the flash winked again. Dell lunged forward, his outstretched hand just touched the flash reflector as the man jerked it away. He was stout and solid with a big speckled oval head, as if he'd been dusted with meal.

'Steady on, mate,' he said. He kept the camera behind his back but didn't budge. 'I was only snatching one in case we got interrupted. There's no one about.'

'What right have you got to come here?' hissed Dell. 'I don't know what you want but get out of here before someone sees you. And give me that film.'

'I said steady on. I tell you there's no one about. Anyway, what's the fuss? I thought it was all fixed up. That's what they said in the office.'

'I don't know what you're talking about. Nothing was fixed with anyone. Put the camera away before I lose my job.'

The photographer sighed. 'You are this bloke Dell, aren't you? For some piece Bob Hunter's writing?'

'There's nothing fixed yet. Now please go. And give me that film.'

'Relax, mate. If the piece isn't used then the pictures won't get used. You don't have to worry. Now while I'm here, let's get one of you at work. Just be having a look inside the bonnet of the car or something. It'll only take a second and I can shoot it from here in the shadow. No one'll see.'

Dell started to turn on his heel and walk away then thought better and faced the man again, scowling. 'Your office will hear about this, I promise you.'

'Sure, sure. Look it won't take a second, and then we'll be shot of this end of the job altogether. You won't need to worry about it again.'

Dell hesitated. A shining new limousine was rolling towards them along the cinder road, pitching gently over the pot-holes. He felt in his overall pocket for the shifting spanner he carried. 'Listen,' he said, 'there's someone coming. Could be one of the directors. I'll pretend to be looking at something but if you aim that camera I'll smash it, I promise you.' He dropped into a crouch and felt for the nearside drive shaft. The limousine slid past and drew up in the middle of the road. Dell sneaked a look. It wasn't anyone in particular.

'Christ,' the photographer was grumbling, 'we went to enough trouble to look after you. Even borrowed this old wreck from one of the reps so that I'd have the right sort of car for this place...'

As Dell started to straighten up the flash winked again. 'You bastard,' he said coldly, and turned and walked away without looking back, all the way to the little red station wagon and the worried man with the ginger moustache. 'Sorry,' he said. 'Somebody trying to throw his weight about. They treat you like dirt, some of these people.'

'Yes, I expect they do,' said the gingery man vaguely. 'You really think I've got to have new suspension boxes?'

'What was that? — I'm sorry.'

'New suspension boxes — do I have to have them?'

Dell made an effort. 'Afraid so. It's just no good trying to patch 'em up on this car. They're made so light that if they go at all they really go.'

'But thirty quid...'

'Well, you know, it's the duty and then the tax on top of the duty. That's the trouble with imported cars.'

'With the other jobs and labour and everything, what would the total damage be?'

'Say forty-five.'

'Well, I could manage it, of course. But I'm wondering if it's worth it. What do you think, Mr. Dell?'

Dell dropped into the jargon of his trade. 'Depends what you want. If it's just a question of keeping yourself mobile, well then, you'll have a vehicle that might last you for another twelve months without trouble. On the other hand, when they get to this stage they sometimes keep on going wrong.'

'I'll put it another way, Mr. Dell. What's the car worth?'

'Seventy-five as it stands, maybe a bit more.'

'*What?* I've seen them like this for a hundred and fifty.'

Dell looked at the windows let not very expertly into the van body, the improvised rear seat. 'Not lately, I doubt. Did you put the windows in yourself?'

'Pal of mine did.'

'And you paid the purchase tax?'

'What purchase tax?'

'What you pay if you convert a van into an estate car. They assess it on the value of the vehicle at the time.'

'I didn't know about that. You live and learn, don't you?' But his voice went light and unconvincing.

Dell shifted his position so that he could read the mileage on the speedometer. He said, 'I'm afraid you'll have a bit of trouble when you come to sell it… It's one of the things they're liable to check on when the registration is transferred.'

'It wouldn't be much to pay now, would it?'

'Well, no. But there might be some awkward questions about when the job was done. I'd be a bit cagey if I were going to buy it.'

'Oh gosh, what next?' He looked comically dismayed.

'You need a vehicle, I take it?'

'Yes, for business. I'm only in a small way, you know, but I'm expanding all the time. It's a big help to be able to get around.'

Dell weighed things up for a second. 'I'll tell you what. I think I know someone who might take it off you, no questions asked. Nothing illegal — he's got a little garage, rebuilds these things for special customers.'

'How much?' said the man dubiously.

'I might be able to get you a hundred.'

'It's only done 30,000, you know. And it's licensed to the end of the year.'

'I'm sorry. A hundred would be the most he'd give.'

'Well, I suppose a hundred to put down would get quite a decent van … He sucked the end of the gingery moustache.

'Oh, indeed. You'd be half way there for an A.30 say two years old — perhaps less.'

'I'll think about it then.'

'Of course, I can't promise anything. The man may not want it any more. Can you leave an address?'

The gingery man carefully unbuttoned a little plastic booklet of visiting cards, detached one and passed it to Dell. It said, South Bucks Woodworm and Dry Rot Eradicators, and in the corner below, Mr. J. H. Doggett and an address and a telephone number in Datchet.

'All right, Mr. Doggett. I'll try and ring you this afternoon either way,' said Dell. 'But it may have to be tomorrow. What times would you be in?'

'Well, it's hard to say. I'm out a lot on the business. But the wife'll always take a message.'

Dell watched him walk away down the cinder road and then called to Stephen. 'Fix the suspension boxes up as well as you can on this old crate,' he said. 'You can drop whatever else you're doing.'

Hunter's car was already backed in behind the holly bush. As Dell pushed his way through the blanket curtain he could hear his voice saying, 'Here's your Daddy. Say hello to Daddy.' It was a good voice, educated and pleasant but with just a hint of a whine in it. Hunter had the baby on his knee, gurgling and grubby. There was a teacup on the table by his elbow and a plate with a biscuit on it. The baby was preoccupied with the teaspoon. Hunter said, 'I didn't mean to beat you to it. I thought you got home a bit earlier than this.'

'That's all right,' said Dell. He called through to the kitchen, 'Baby not bathed yet?'

'Just going in.' Nancy appeared. She'd her apron on and her face was a bit flushed. She wobbled slightly on unaccustomed high heels. 'Come on, Miss.' She heaved the baby up. It grabbed her round the neck, burying its face in her cardigan, and kicking with fat pink legs. Nancy turned away so that it should see Dell over her shoulder. 'Who's that, then? Eh?'

The baby pointed a fat forefinger and said, 'Da-de.'

'Did she get her jab?'

'Yes she did. And so far she's none the worse for it, thank goodness.' They disappeared into the kitchen. The door swung to after them. There was the sound of a kettle of water being added to the bath. Dell hung up his mac and scarf.

Hunter said, 'I think there's some tea still in the pot.'

'Thanks, I'll wait.'

'I was hoping you and Mrs. Dell would perhaps come out and have a meal with me, but she says she can't leave the children. So she very kindly asked me to stay and have something with you...'

36

'Oh,' said Dell. 'Did she? Perhaps I'd better have a cup after all.' He helped himself, and as an afterthought reached for the biscuit on the plate by Hunter's elbow.

Hunter looked at the fire, bigger and more blazing than Dell usually kept it. He said, 'This really is a cosy little place. I've friends in London who'd go crazy about it. Of course, you've no electricity but I think that's rather an attraction. A good excuse not to watch television … no telephone … marvellous…'

Dell drank his tea.

Hunter tried again. 'I've often thought I'd like to find a country cottage for myself. Come down at the weekend for a long sleep, cut the hedges, write a chapter of the novel…'

Dell said, 'Your photographer didn't waste much time.'

'Oh?' Hunter looked genuinely surprised. 'Where was that?'

'At the works. Could have been very awkward for me indeed. He even had a flash gun.'

'Gosh, I'm sorry. The idiots! I'm afraid I've no control over that side. I'll certainly complain, though.'

Two more minutes ticked by. From the kitchen came the sounds of baby talk and the baby's little quacking voice. Hunter leaned over the arm of his chair and peered at Dell's bookshelves, twisting his head on one side to read the titles. 'Auden … Isherwood … Barker … maths, more maths, chess problems … Angus Wilson … Koestler … all those Penguins.' He glanced at Dell. 'Quite a Catholic assortment for a motor mechanic?'

'That's a silly, snobby remark.'

'I'm sorry. It's not my day.' The sad upper lip folded over the lower one again. He was good-looking in a rather passive way, dark hair making a little widow's peak in the middle of his forehead; under the dark overcoat which he'd kept on but unbuttoned he wore a dark suit. The panels of his tie alternately glinted and lay matt. He said, 'Did you think any more about the — er — proposition?'

The kitchen door banged open and Nancy brought the baby through, ready for bed. 'What do you say?'

The baby thought for a moment, eyes even brighter than her bright pink face, and said, 'Ni-ni —'

'There's a good girl.'

'Jolly good,' said Hunter. 'Sleep well.' He waited until Nancy had clattered down the stairs again and gone into the kitchen to clear up. He looked down at Dell. 'Well?'

Upstairs the baby stopped bouncing its bottom and started to cry. Hunter looked perplexed.

'It's all right,' said Dell. 'It's only a kind of resistance to sleep, a clinging on to consciousness. When you're that age you don't know about sleep. Consciousness is all you know. You want to hang on to it. This home and this family is what I want to hang on to. Does that answer your question?' Without waiting for a reply he called through to the kitchen, 'What time did you say we'll be eating, Nan?'

'Whatever time you like. Only it'll take me a while to cook.'

Dell pushed himself away from the table. 'You've got your car outside? Let's go to the pub and have a talk.'

Tony said. 'Who's that man that came?' He was back in bed but he said he'd been up until teatime. He looked better.

'Just a man who wants to see me.'

'Uh.' He accepted that. 'Did he come in a car?'

'The car you saw yesterday. You drew a picture of it.'

'Where's the car now?'

'It's by the shed. You can't quite see it from here but if you look out of the window it'll go by in a minute. I'm going with the man and we're coming back later. I'll say good night now, because you'll be asleep by then.'

'Daddy, can we have a bonfire for Guy Fawkes?'

'I'll see. Say good night now.'

'When is Guy Fawkes?'

'It should be November the fifth but this year that's a Sunday so people have their bonfires and fireworks on Saturday, which is November the *fourth*.'

'What's today?'

Dell thought. 'November the first.'

'Did you say Ratsandrabbits?'

'No, I forgot.'

'I diddunt. I said it.'

'Go on with you. You just asked what day it is.' He pushed his fingers through Tony's hair that sometimes looked as if it were going grey already and turned to go.

'I did,' said Tony after him. 'I betchou I did.'

After one drink and mid-way through the second Dell said, 'Excuse me a sec. I want to make a phone call.' Hunter's face went wary. 'It's a customer at the garage. I promised him I'd let him know about his car.'

The wary looked relaxed a bit. 'I'll get you another drink. What's it to be?'

'The same, thanks.'

'Pint?'

'Just a half'll do.'

There was a telephone behind the bar but so was there a Cobb. Dell went out of the pub and round the bend in the top road to the public call box two hundred yards away. It stood all alone, not a house in sight. Dell had never found out why they'd put it there or who it was supposed to serve. Inside it smelled damp and pissy. He struck a match and ranged a sixpence, a shilling and four pennies on top of the coin box, then stared at the printed instructions, his eye reading them, his attention elsewhere. The flame burned down. In the dark he covered one of the pennies with his hand and struck another match and looked at the penny. Heads. He pushed it into the slot and the remaining three after it. The number turned out to be a local call. No more to pay. A woman's voice answered, thin and off-hand.

'Is Mr. Doggett there please?'

No reply. He remembered to push the button, and tried again.

'Yes, just a minute.' There was a pause, then 'Hullo.' The careful drawl was new to Dell.

'It's Dell here. From the works.'

'Oh yes.' The drawl vanished.

'About your little vehicle...' Dell paused, waiting for encouragement. None came. 'It'll be ready tomorrow.'

'Oh, splendid.'

'That chap I mentioned —I think he would definitely be interested.'

'Well, I haven't really thought about it enough yet...'

'He'd only be interested if he could have it straight away.'

'You mean like next week?'

'Tomorrow, more like.'

'Can I ring you back on this?'

'No, I'll ring you.'

'All right. Listen, Mr. Dell...'

'Yes.'

'I think it'll be a deal. Don't bother to ring. I'll see you at the garage tomorrow.'

Dell hurried back to the pub. Hunter was watching the door anxiously. He said relievedly, 'I was beginning to think you'd decided to deliver the message by hand.'

'I thought I'd better go along the road to the box. They don't like you using the phone here.' Dell found he was slightly out of breath. He lifted his refilled glass. 'Cheers.'

'Cheers,' said Hunter. He added casually, 'That's a middle-class thing to say.'

'What is?'

'Cheers.'

'There you go again. Trying to prove something or other.' But there was no impatience in his voice. The pub had mysteriously become warm and friendly. The drink was welcoming. He said, 'This man I'm supposed to be — did he like a drink?'

'He liked a beer according to the cuttings I read.'

'I thought they were all supposed to be drunks or homosexuals or Communists.'

'Not necessarily. They could have been idealists, convinced that what they were doing was the right thing. Couldn't they?'

Dell said, 'I knew a scientist once, in the army. Well, not exactly in the army. In the Home Guard, more. He was the same as anyone else except…'

'Except what?'

'Oh, nothing. Look, supposing you were to find this man, wouldn't you have to report him to the police or the security people?'

'Why? There's no warrant out for him, there never was. No one has ever said for sure there's anything against him. All he did was disappear while investigations were going on.'

'Which was damning in itself, surely?'

'Well, obviously it looked bad. But the whole Longbow project was wound up a couple of years later and the security scandal was well and truly eclipsed by the political squabble. Besides, the climate was easier then —' He stopped short.

'And now it's not. We're in the age of the witch-hunt.' Dell shook his head. 'That man would be crazy to own up to anything.'

Hunter said, 'In which case we'd probably go ahead on our own.'

'Would you dare?'

'It would depend on the lawyer.'

Dell weighed that up. 'If the man were to co-operate, how soon would the article appear?'

'The series starts on Sunday but this particular story mightn't be used for weeks yet. You can't tell…'

'And what would the man be expected to do? Wait for it to be printed? Hang on and wait for the police and the Security and all the other newspapers like yours to come swarming round?'

Hunter thought for a moment. 'That would probably be unwise of him … officially, of course, we wouldn't have to know anything about any plans to skip — you know, aiding and abetting. Unofficially we'd help him, I should think.'

'How very decent of you!' Hunter blinked at the change in tone. 'You'd help him. How very decent. You'd help him abandon his home, his job, all he's got, and take off into the nowhere. Where's he supposed to go, what's he supposed to live on? How far is a hundred stinking quid supposed to go?' The vehemence subsided as quickly as it had risen. He finished lamely, 'I wanted you to try and see what you do to people in your job.'

Hunter revolved his glass in the wet on the table, looking down at the patterns he made. He said, 'It's not all like that. When I got off news on to features I thought it would never be like that again.'

'If you found a man like the one I'm supposed to be and then let him go, what would happen then?'

'To me personally? I'd get the sack. But I told you, they have the address and everything in the office. They started it, not me. If I dropped out, someone else would come in.'

Dell drank up. 'We'd better go.'

Hunter said, 'Wait for me in the car. I just want to get something.' When he came out of the pub he was carrying a couple of bottles.

'That was very good indeed.' said Hunter. He took a gulp of wine from the tumbler. Nancy had cooked a mixed grill of bacon, liver, two lamb chops, tomatoes, and even a few mushrooms. The wine came from one of the bottles Hunter had brought back; the other was a half of Scotch. Hunter had eaten quickly, rather untidily. The moment he'd finished he lit a cigarette.

'I'm sorry there isn't any more,' said Nancy. She glowed in the lamplight, warmed by the wine and the unusualness of company. 'But there's a bit of cheese. And a tart I made. Won't you have a piece then?' Her posh voice was in full operation.

'No, no. That was marvellous, that's all I want.' He turned his head to blow smoke out away from the table. 'Living on my own, I don't eat much, you know.'

Dell cut a piece of bacon in two and speared one half, along with his last piece of liver. He drank some more of the wine and looked at the label on the bottle, Macon. He said, 'I went through Macon once.'

Hunter said, 'Really? When was that?'

'With a W.T.A. Tour. In 1950.'

'Eh?' said Nancy. 'You never told me about that.'

'Does he tell you about himself before you were married, Mrs. Dell?'

'Not a lot.'

'You won't get far that way,' said Dell.

'Listen,' said Nancy. 'What is all this about? What's going on with you two?'

Dell rubbed a piece of bread and butter in the grease on his plate. 'Mr. Hunter thinks I was once a scientist and a traitor called Bristow who managed to disappear. In fact, he's offering two hundred pounds for the story, supplied by me, written by him!'

Nancy looked from one face to the other. 'I don't know where he could have got hold of such a thing. It's barmy…' To Hunter she said, 'You've got the wrong feller.'

Dell said, 'The two hundred would be useful, though.'

She looked at him blankly, then got up. 'I'll fetch the sweet.'

In a minute, Dell knew, she'd call him. She did, ostensibly to bring his plate. In the kitchen she hooked the door to with her foot. 'I don't know what you're playing at, but don't.' Her face was set. 'Don't fool about with what we've got, Dell, because we'd never get it again and you know that.'

'It's not so simple as you think. He's got it pretty well watertight.'

'For God's sake, are you going to let us be crucified by some newspaper fellow? It's not just you, you know. It's all of us. Me, Tony, the girl. What happens? Are we supposed just to pack up one night and settle down again somewhere else, just like that? Anyway, the boy's not fit to go. He'd not stand it.'

'Listen, there's nothing we can do about it. You've always known about me, that we'd always have this hanging over us. Just because the last three years it's been easy doesn't mean it's all over…'

'Okay, okay, but you don't have to take it lying down! Fight him! Don't let him just get away with it. Don't — don't *flirt* with the fellow, with your talk of a couple of hundred pounds being useful.'

'Sssh.' Her voice had risen. 'I tell you he's got it all tied up. It's not only him, there's others on his paper. They've got proof, they reckon. They've only got to breathe the word … I'm just trying to get the best for us, that's all.' She stared up at him, legs braced apart, nostrils dilated. She was breathing very deeply, perhaps on purpose. Dell held her gaze. She said abruptly, 'Was the meal nice?'

'Very nice.'

'Good. That was the kid's chops for tomorrow's dinner. I'll have to get them something different now.'

'I'll give you a bit extra,' said Dell hurriedly. He went back into the front room.

'Right,' said Hunter. 'If we get going now…' He rummaged among the folded papers in his pocket for a clean piece. 'I'll only note down dates and names and things. A story like this should tell itself.'

Nancy had gone to bed. The fire blazed. Dell was sprawled on the old sofa. Hunter sat in the armchair. The whisky and two glasses and some water in a blue and white milk jug were between them. Hunter poured two generous ones.

'For a start,' he said, 'how did you do it? How did you just disappear? Where did you go? This is virgin territory. In all the cuttings the facts stop in July '54 and from there on it's just surmise. Colour stories about the peaceful country town whose inhabitants never speculated about what went on up at the valve works. Background on the popular, brilliant Dr. Cliente, pillar of the local music society and leading boffin until he shot himself in a hotel room in Milan. Background on the brilliant John Bristow, who liked a pint and a game of bar billiards with the locals. Background on retired garage proprietor George Bristow who disowned his son but had short shrift with reporters and sympathisers. Or on Bristow's fiancée, pretty, talented Stella Rayner who'd waited for him in vain at the Gare du Nord in Paris, the tickets in her pocket for a romantic holiday in Spain...'

'All right, all right. You don't need to go on. I saw most of it at the time. Including the innuendoes about the romantic holiday going to be with Cliente rather than with any girl.'

Hunter looked uncomfortable. 'I wasn't on the story myself then. I hadn't got to London. I was still in Glasgow covering fires and sermons.'

'Glasgow? You were warmer than you knew. It was Glasgow I skipped from. The nearest I went to the Continent was the Spanish consulate to get a visa. People obligingly assumed the rest. I went to Glasgow and got the boat to Belfast. It was the Friday night at the start of Glasgow Fair and the boat was solid with drunks and fights. Joe Stalin could have walked off the other end without them noticing. A little walk across the border into Eire and you ought to be able to guess the rest.'

'Well, we started to once we had the story about the Irish documents. But that's brand new information. Nobody ever suspected Ireland before. How did you manage? What did you do?'

'I had a friend at Trinity who put me up. He only had a room in one of those ropy old Georgian houses, but he was coming up to his last year as a medical and he was most of his time at the hospital. He went home to England in August for four weeks and I gave him those letters to post at London Airport. I stayed on in his room until the beginning of term in October. I lived on about a quid a week. I used to make a big pan of spaghetti at the beginning of the week, with tinned stew and tinned tomatoes and eat that, one meal a day, plus a few cups of tea. Work was out of the question, of course, at least for the time being. I didn't have any permit or anything, and anyway the Irish have to leave home to get work themselves. Later someone said to try Shannon and I had some casual jobs at the airport there, the kind that students could get, nothing that lasted. Still, I managed to hang on till the end of the year. Crossed back to Liverpool on Boxing Night, I always picked the times the boats were crowded and full of drunks. I remember walking along the North Wall to the boat because I didn't have the bus fare left, and my shoes let in the wet and I'd had Christmas Day all on my own — sausages, potato crisps and a cupful of flat Guinness I found in the bottom of a screw top.'

'That's it!' Hunter was jubilant. 'That's the kind of detail that makes a story come to life. There's almost an angle there about the time you've had being tougher than any prison sentence you might have got. Seven Years Hard. My Self-imposed Seven Years Hard…' He drained his glass. 'Your wife, what about her? You met her in Liverpool?'

'In a Yates wine lodge, if that's what you're after. But she doesn't come into your story. That was later. You want to know what happened in 1954. I'm telling you.'

'We have to bring it up to date. After all, the series is going to be called Where Are They Now? What are the children's names and how old are they?'

'Oh God. The baby's supposed to be called Amanda but we haven't got round to it yet. She's nearly a year. Tony's six. You know about him.'

'Yes.' Hunter put on a solemn face. 'Does he go to school?'

'He was supposed to have started this term but he's only been about three weeks out of eight. I try and teach him a bit at the weekends.'

'While we're on the subject,' said Hunter, 'your own background isn't awfully well documented.' He was getting through the whisky methodically and his face began to look blotchy, even in the yellowy light of the lamps and the fire. 'Your schooldays, for instance. Or your parents. Your mother died in the war, I think.'

'Yes,' said Dell shortly.

'Your father's still alive. Married again. You don't have any contact…?'

'None. He's disowned me, like you said.'

'Of course he was upset at the time. But have you tried lately?'

'He didn't understand then. He wouldn't now. He wouldn't ever.'

'Other people would?'

Dell looked up. 'I don't know. I don't much care. You have to do what seems right to you, that's all.'

Hunter flung out his arm, an unlit cigarette between the fingers. 'This is it! This is what we haven't touched on at all, the Why of the business. We've got the How but not the Why.' He searched for a match. 'You know, the *anatomy* of betrayal. What made you do it?'

'Does it matter?'

'Of course it matters! We've offered you a chance to defend yourself directly to three million readers. That's not to be sneezed at, especially if…'

'If what?'

'Well, if there were any repercussions.'

'Repercussions! There'll be repercussions all right.'

'Not necessarily,' Hunter tried to retrieve himself. 'It's seven years ago now. Do you remember Edwards, the special branch man?'

'I'm hardly likely to forget him. Puffing round the place with that old pipe going.'

'I met him last weekend. Got the crime man to take me along to the pub he uses. Of course we didn't say we were on to you. Just making Sunday pub-time conversation. He's very cagey; never gives anything away. But I got the impression they weren't very sore about you any more. In fact I had to remind him of your name.'

'I can't chance it.'

'Where will you go, then?'

Dell thought for a moment. 'Back to Ireland. Only this time to stay, I suppose. There's no extradition for this kind of thing, I believe.'

'Perhaps that would be wisest,' said Hunter. He reached for his glass. 'You still haven't told me why you did it. You weren't in the C.P. or so they said.'

'A Communist, you mean? No I wasn't anything, much.' He drank more deeply of his drink than he had before, pulling a face at the aftertaste. 'I was just pretty impressionable, I think. I used to listen to Left people I knew and it was very exciting and I'd want to go along with them and kick the King out of the Palace or something. Then other times I'd listen to the reactionaries and I'd feel a kind of pull, that it was with them I belonged, I'd been born and brought up in their lot and I'd never be able to be anything else…'

Hunter looked disappointed. 'Well, yes, but can you be more specific? When was this, where? Was there any special person? Was it Cliente?'

'No, it wasn't Cliente, poor sod. It goes back further than that … I had a tutor at Cambridge…'

'Just a sec,' said Hunter. He was sitting on the edge of the settee. 'I think I'll have to go somewhere. I'm bursting.'

'It's out the back. But go anywhere, it doesn't matter. We don't grow anything much.' He remembered the torch and called after Hunter but he'd already gone. Dell stared into the fire and worried a sliver of hard, loose skin on his thumb. The moment Hunter re-appeared he said, 'No it wasn't Cambridge really, it was earlier, at school which I hated. It was in the war, you see, and everybody was as patriotic as hell. Well, I wanted to be patriotic, too, and go off and fight and come back to the school on leave, in a second-lieutenant's uniform or something. But meanwhile I was only fifteen, and at fifteen I had to choose which sixth form I was going in. I liked arts, I was good at English, exceptionally good, I got an A in School Cert., if you remember School Cert. —'

'Of course,' said Hunter vaguely. His voice was thicker and his face blotchier. The cold air outside had had its effect. He lowered himself into the chair again and grabbed his glass.

'On the other hand I'd also done well in maths and physics. Actually, I'd done well in quite a lot of things. The headmaster said that the English was only an essay — those were his words: only an essay. And as I'd done well in science it was patriotic duty to go into the science sixth, because the country would need scientists. It made sense to my old man, too, because it sounded more practical. It was only my mum who ever took an interest in what I liked doing, and she was dead.'

Hunter manoeuvred his head up and down in heavy sympathy.

'So I went into the science sixth, and I did quite well, and the headmaster put me in for a thing called a State Bursary, which again it was my patriotic duty to accept, implying that the boys who were better at games would stand more chance of winning the school a V.C. on the battlefield. I was a likelier investment as a potential First at one of the Older Universities. So I went to Cambridge at government expense and worked like hell to get through the Natural Sciences Tripos in two years instead of three, and all the time the feeling that I was under some irredeemable obligation to everyone, indentured to the country for the rest of my life. Anyway, I got a First and the war ended that summer and now that it was all over they put me in the Air Force as a technical officer; a Wingless Wonder, my father kindly called me.' Hunter's eyes were drooping. 'But I'm boring you.'

'No, no, go on.' Hunter jerked himself upright.

'Well, when I got to the Research Establishment in 1950 as a full-blown scientific officer, grade one, I found I was still supposed to be under some obligation. If ever I complained about anything the director used to say, 'You realise your parents would have had to spend a small fortune to give you the education you've had.' As a matter of fact I was on a career income of £48,000 counting in all the statutory increments. At the time it was about £900 a year.'

'Doesn't sound bad to me,' said Hunter. 'At least you didn't have to bugger people around for a living, like I do. You weren't dependent on the whim of some ignorant news editor. You had security.'

'Security, we had that all right. We might have been working on the original atom bomb. And what was it? — the thing that all the trouble was about? It was a missile-homing device that never homed a single bloody missile, because the missile in question got scrubbed before it ever got fired. But I could see an application development to make a little emergency navigator for civil aircraft. Cheap, foolproof, just the thing for backward countries. And I wasn't even allowed to write a paper on the theory, leaving out the specific electronics! Something that could save lives, help the world a bit and they looked at me as if I'd been caught repairing television sets in office time or something.'

Hunter struggled with his bits of paper. He was alert again. 'Hey, wait a minute. Is that it? You wanted to go on with this safety device, save peoples' lives instead of working on weapons. So when they wouldn't let you, you secretly contacted someone who you thought would develop it, not realising — or perhaps not caring — that it would mean the information going to the other side?'

'God, not as simple as that. Things are never clear-cut that way. I don't suppose anything would ever have happened if I hadn't been sent to Cliente's place to work with him. He had the contacts. Had been doing his bit towards the free exchange of scientific information for some time. Only it was political in his case ... I suppose in mine it was just the need to do something to justify the lousy career I'd never wanted...'

'Yes, yes,' said Hunter. He wasn't listening. He'd got what he wanted and was closed to further complications. He stuffed the bundle of papers and envelopes into his pocket and looked at his watch. 'Golly, the time.'

Dell said, 'You don't want to start driving back to London now. You can sleep on the sofa if you like. I'll find some blankets.'

'If you're sure you don't mind…'

When Dell brought the blankets downstairs he said, as casually as he could, 'You must have seen Stella Rayner recently.'

'Who? Oh, yes — only a week ago.'

'How is she?'

'All right. Not very forthcoming. Still, very loyal to you — you should be flattered. She let me borrow the letters after some persuasion but wouldn't talk much.'

'She's not bitter, then?'

'No-o-h. Her father seems to have a bit of a chip on his shoulder, but not her … she went back to live with them and teaches nippers in the local school. The mother was in hospital. I didn't see her.'

Dell said, mainly to himself, 'She was the one that jumped to conclusions; if you as much as took Stella to the pictures she started planning the reception.'

CHAPTER 3: THURSDAY

Dell ran his tongue over coated teeth and made a face at the taste in his mouth and closed his eyes and sought oblivion again. Nancy said, 'Don't go back to sleep. You've still got to go to work, you know.' Later, it was her voice calling from below and the baby starting to cry in response that woke him for a second time. Downstairs the living room smelled stale and cold. Hunter was on the settee still, his overcoat on top of the blankets. He was propped up on one elbow smoking the first cigarette of the day, a cup of tea by his side. His stubble was very dark. He said, 'Good morning. How you feeling?'

Dell went slowly into his grate-keeping routine. The hearth and surround were deep in cigarette ash. Nancy, hurrying down with the baby, said, 'Leave that, you're not going to get your bus. Better have some breakfast.'

Hunter said, 'Couldn't I run your husband to work? That would give more time.'

'It's all right,' said Dell. 'I'll manage.'

'No, no. It's the least I can do after imposing on you like this. I mean, staying the night.'

'Go on, let him, love,' said Nancy. 'It'll save a rush.' To Hunter she added, 'You'd better borrow my husband's razor. You can't go round looking like Bluebeard.' To Dell again, 'Tone's better again this morning. I'll get him up after breakfast.'

While Hunter warmed up the engine Dell darted back into the cottage. 'Don't forget,' he whispered, 'your Mum's worse. Tell them in the shops.'

As they bumped down the bridle path the infinitely corrupt smell of the mink farm wafted in strongly. Hunter wound up the window and said, 'I could do without that, this morning especially.'

Dell smiled at a recollection. 'Nancy and I were on the way to the pub the other evening — the evening you first turned up. It was pretty powerful then, too. Nance said quite seriously, "Hey do you think it could be affecting Tony?"'

Hunter laughed dutifully, then just as dutifully let the smile fade. 'What exactly is the trouble with him?'

'Oh, I don't know. It's sort of nervous, really. He's never been right. He was a forceps delivery, some ham-fisted student in Walton Hospital. When he runs his legs go all ways.'

'Perhaps he'll grow out of it. And they're making great strides all the time, you know, in this field.'

'Yes, sure,' said Dell.

'He seems bright, from what I hear.'

'Yes.'

On the main road Hunter cleared his throat and said, 'I've been thinking some more about what you could do once the story's out. There's a cottage in Wiltshire we used once before, miles from anywhere. It belongs to the man in New York.'

'How's that any different from where we are now?'

'Where you are now, it wouldn't take the other papers five minutes to get on to you. I mean, you'd be recognised by the locals straightaway. It'd be pretty tough. Not only on you. On the wife and kids, too.'

'Besides which, your paper wouldn't have us to itself any more.'

'I won't deny that element comes into it. We're not philanthropists. But look at it from your point of view. It depends how much public interest in you there turns out to be.

I think it might be considerable and there's another little proposition I could make, a more personal one. A book. You know, the full story, all that detail that's so good. Maybe some title developed from that point I made last night. We could work on it together … you hinted you'd have liked a literary career.'

'Oh God,' said Dell. 'Not that way!'

'It could make a lot of money. Serial rights. I could maybe get an advance of five hundred.'

'Thanks for the thought, anyway.'

They drove on in silence broken only by directions from Dell. At the entrance to the trading estate he said, 'This'll do. You'd better not take me any further. People might see.'

'Yes, okay.'

'When do I get the hundred?'

'I'll try and get it for you today. Listen, I'm going to phone the office from somewhere round here. They might want me to stay out this way. Silly to drive all the way into the town and then come back. But I'll try and get the money sent. Where can I find you?'

'Whatever happens, don't come to the works. Your photographer nearly finished me yesterday.'

'All right but where then?'

Dell thought for a minute. 'I don't ever go out for a drink in the lunch-break so I'd better not start now. But' — he pointed — 'just round the corner there there's a little betting shop. You can't miss it, big electric sign. I sometimes nip out there.'

'What time?'

'Say 12.15.'

'Okay.'

Doggett the Woodworm man was waiting by the office.

'You're bright and early,' said Dell.

'You said last night it'd be ready.'

'It is, all bar a road test.'

'Can't wait for that. Got a big survey up Wycombe way.'

Dell looked at him anxiously. 'What time would you be finished? I told that fellow I might be able to show him the little vehicle today.'

'Business first, Mr. Dell. You know that. But I should be through by afternoon. I'll look in on my way back if you like.'

By noon Dell had been to the lavatory four times, but it wasn't just the after-effects of the night before. He examined himself in the mirror over the washroom basin. There was a cold, drawn look to his face that matched the cold, drawn symptoms inside him. He held out his hand and it trembled. The noise as someone opened the door with his elbow gave him a sick, jerky feeling that he couldn't localise. The incomer, holding his oily hands like claws ready to nudge on a tap with the same elbow, raised his eyebrows.

'Feeling all right?'

'Yes, thanks. Had a bit too much last night.'

'And the best of luck, mate.'

Hunter's car and another stood outside the betting shop. Inside Hunter and the mealy-headed photographer from the day before were bent over the racing edition of an evening paper, but Hunter looked up immediately, as if he hadn't really been engrossed.

'Just as well you're here,' he said cheerily. 'We've got ten bob on the two thirty already and now he fancies something in the next race.'

'Hi,' said Mealy-head.

Dell nodded at him coldly. He scanned the place quickly to make sure there was no one from the works in yet. He'd set an early hour especially. Everyone would still be in the canteen.

Hunter was watching him. 'Would you rather talk somewhere else?'

'If you don't mind.'

'Let's go for a drive round in the car.' As they pulled away from the kerb, he said over his shoulder, 'Have you got the doings, Joe?' The photographer produced a sealed envelope from inside his overcoat. Hunter passed it directly to Dell. 'Here you are. A hundred. Before Joe there puts it on some elderly horse.'

'Thanks,' said Dell.

'Now look, two things have happened. I'm not supposed to tell you — I'll get shot if they knew — but there's an idea in the office they want to run this story on Sunday —'

'*This* Sunday?'

'Yes. As a news story, without waiting for the feature. It seems crazy to me but they're afraid someone else will get on to it; also there's some big security debate coming up in the House. Also they're a bit short of news this week. They want you to lead the paper.'

Dell stared at him. 'I had a feeling something like this was happening,' he muttered.

Hunter ignored him. In the presence of a colleague he was more the newspaperman. 'The other thing is that Joe here's got to get some more pictures. It's all right, not at the factory — the ones he took yesterday will do. Some at home, of the cottage and Mrs. Dell and the kids.'

'That's right,' said Mealy-head. 'If we could get them sort of packing up to flee, something like that.'

'The point is,' said Hunter, 'that they need to be in daylight, really.'

'Especially the one of them turning to have a last look at the cottage that's been their home for seven years,' said Mealy-head.

'Three years,' said Dell. 'It was only three years in the cottage. We were in other places before.' He stared blankly at a woman waiting at a bus-stop.

'If you could give him a note or something,' said Hunter. 'So's Mrs. Dell would know it was all right I ought to get back to the office myself.'

Dell nodded, trying to think, trying to plan. They were back outside the betting shop. Hunter stopped the car. Mealy-head leaned forward with a notebook, open ready, and a ballpoint pen. It was a change from Hunter's scraps of paper, anyway. Dell thought for a moment and wrote, 'This is the photographer from the paper, Sweetie. Do what he says within reason — no mucking about with the kids. Don't say anything at all. I'll be home as soon as I can.' He tore out the sheet and folded it in six and tucked one flap under another, like they'd done at school years before.

Mealy-head put it away with ostentatious incuriosity. 'With luck,' he said, 'I'll be back this way in time to pick up the winnings.'

When he'd clambered out of the car and into his own, Hunter said, urgently, sibilantly, 'Now how about the Wiltshire cottage? I didn't want to say anything about it in front of him. You can't trust photographers. They use the same dark room and what have you as the boys on the Daily. They're always gossiping, too. I wouldn't be surprised to see the Daily on to the story *before* Sunday if we aren't careful...'

Dell shouted, 'What do you mean? What are you driving at?'

'All right. Relax. It's pretty safe, but there's always a risk. Now could you be ready first thing tomorrow morning? I'll drive you there myself if I can get away. Otherwise it'll be a hire-car, very cosy.'

'But what about supplies and things?'

'Couldn't you stop on the way somewhere?'

'You don't understand.' Dell heard the exasperation mounting in his voice. 'What about a cot for the baby? Does your cottage have a cot? A bed for the boy? Something to boil nappies in?'

'Gosh, I never thought of that. There are beds enough, a copper out the back, I think. But a cot … you couldn't take yours?'

'It's hardly very portable.'

'Well, we'd have to try, and if it wouldn't go we'd have to get another one there. Don't *make* difficulties.'

Dell said, 'I'll have to get back now.'

'Well, what do you think?'

'I just don't know.'

'Hadn't you better decide?'

Dell bit his lip. 'You don't think Ireland would be better?'

'I told you. We couldn't have any part in it, helping someone leave the country. Try it on your own if you must but don't expect any help. My advice is to stay in this country and face the music if necessary.'

'I don't know if I could, any more.' It wasn't much more than a whisper. Hunter looked at him momentarily, then somewhere down at the pedals. The briskness went out of his voice. 'I'm sorry. I've been blathering on. Christ, how I hate this job.'

Dell pushed the door open and got out of the car. He said, 'You'd better come, then. Tomorrow morning.'

It was three o'clock before Doggett the Woodworm man returned. Dell drew him out of any possible earshot. He said, 'I've got the money if you're still interested.'

Doggett fingered the end of his ginger moustache. 'I s'pose so. Actually the little bus has been running beautifully today … still, a deal's a deal, isn't it? The only thing is I'd been counting on her again tomorrow.'

Dell worked hard to sound casual. 'I don't think the chap would wait another day. You know, if he doesn't get started tomorrow it won't be worth starting Saturday morning and before he knows where he is, it's Monday and he's lost three whole days.'

'All right,' said Doggett reasonably. 'You said a hundred and five?'

'A hundred,' said Dell. 'But I'll make it a hundred and five for delivery today.'

'That's fair, very fair indeed,' said Doggett. 'Of course I've got my stuff aboard at the moment. And you'll need the registration book.'

'Sure, sure. Take it home. Unload at your leisure. But if I could have it at, say, five o'clock.'

'Cando.'

'Not here, though,' said Dell quickly. 'They wouldn't be keen on me mixing private business and their business, if you understand…'

'Of course.'

'Do you know the Ritz picture house? — that's not far from your part of the world, is it? There's a car park round the side. Five o'clock, then?'

'I'll be there.'

Dell turned to go back into the service shop. The works manager was coming straight for him. Dell swivelled on his heel, pretending he'd forgotten something, cursing himself under his breath at the same time for a stupid guilt laden trick.

'Mr. Dell!'

'Yessir.'

'I thought that little vehicle went out this morning.'

'It did. We gave the customer an estimate for the work that needed to be done. He thought it was too high. Came back to say he'd decided to sell it instead. Wanted to know if we'd be interested.'

'I hope you told him we wouldn't.'

'Yessir.'

'But politely, Mr. Dell.'

'Very politely.'

'Splendid.' The works manager gave an abrupt smile and headed for the stores. Dell watched him disappear, said to himself, 'Now's as good a time as ever' and ducked behind the workshop bay and past the Not-for-resale petrol pumps to the side road where there was a telephone box. Before the betting shop had opened there'd always been a furtive queue of workers outside. Now Dell got in without delay. He leafed through the directory and made his call and was back in the shop within ten minutes.

They brought the wages packets round starting at four. Dell fidgeted and manoeuvred to catch the cashier's eye early. The cashier made a tiny ceremony of it, weighing the packet in his hand, twinkling. He said, 'A bit heavier this week, Mr. Dell. At this rate you'll be on a monthly salary before you know where you are, or if my experience is anything to go by, a monthly overdraft.'

Dell laughed dutifully. 'I'll cross that one when I come to it.' He shoved the packet unopened into his pocket, next to the thick envelope Hunter had given him and set off on a brisk tour of all jobs in hand. None of them seemed likely to produce any snags before knocking-off time. At 4.35 he cut through the little passage to the side road again and walked unhurriedly away from the works, not looking round at all, still in his brown overall coat, but with his jacket on underneath. His old mac he'd have to forfeit. At the limits of the trading estate he took off the overall, rolled it up and carried it under his arm. The sky was overcast. It was nearly dark already.

Dell stopped at the biggest, busiest garage on the way home and filled up with petrol. Oil and tyres would have been checked at the works the day before. As Doggett had said, the tiny motor was running well. He approached the cottage along the top road, switching off his lights as he turned quickly into the bridle path. The elastic suspension smoothed out the bumps. Dell peered anxiously through the grey trees into the mink farm in case anyone was about. He saw no one. At the cottage he left the motor running while he jumped out and struggled with the sagging, derelict double doors to the old shed.

'Hey, it's Dad, Mum, with a car!' Dell heard Tony's erratic footsteps fractionally before his excited voice. Then Nancy was saying, 'What are you doing home already?'

'Never mind now,' said Dell urgently. 'And not so loud. Do you want everyone to hear? Help me with these doors.' He got the car in, switched off and they started to heave the doors back into position. The first came soggily away from its hinges altogether. 'As long as it hides the car it'll do,' said Dell.

'Is it ours, Dad?'

'You could say it was.'

Nancy stopped jerking at the other door and stepped inside the shed and touched the thin metal wheel housing and sniffed the smell of warm oil. 'Go on,' she said. 'It's not really ours.'

'It is.'

Her eyes shone. 'Our own car? Honest?'

'Yes, but come on, we've got to get cracking.' They pushed at the door. Tony ran to and fro between house and shed on the tips of his toes, agog. Dell put his arm round Nancy's shoulder. He said, 'Things aren't too good, Nance. We have to be moving.'

'What happened then?'

'They're likely to put it all in their damned paper this Sunday.'

'But he said —'

'What that sort of man says isn't worth a light It's going to be Sunday now, may be even sooner. He was dropping hints that their daily bloody paper might jump the gun. It's all the same firm.'

They were inside now. 'I'll get you a cup,' said Nancy, heading for the kitchen.

'No time for that.' Dell felt a tugging at his trousers. He looked down. The baby was hauling herself to her feet, beaming at him from a jammy face. He reached down and rubbed the warm little head. 'There's a hire car coming from Ward's at six-thirty to take you and the kids to Reading —'

'*What!*'

'Please, just listen. It's not a real journey, it's a blind. I've got it all worked out. It's been half worked out for years. The car takes you to Reading and if the driver wants to know where I am you can say I'm meeting you there, coming by train from work. But don't say anything unless he asks. You don't have to pay him, they send a bill in later. At Reading you book two adult and one half, second class, to Dublin by the Fishguard route. We'll assume the baby goes free. There's twenty-five pounds in an envelope here, you shouldn't need half that. The train's at seven-thirty something but you don't catch it. You get on the wrong platform and you get the diesel just about the same time back this way. Here are the tickets. They're day returns I just bought. Throw away the outward halves first. I'll meet you with the car at Maidenhead.'

Nancy looked despairingly round the cluttered living room. 'But I've nothing ready.'

'What about the getaway bags?'

'They haven't been kept up the past two years.'

'Then they should have been. But it doesn't matter. I told you, you're coming back. As long as you've got *some* luggage with you. I can start sorting out the rest while you've gone. Have the kids finished their tea? Get them cleaned up and into warm clothes. Better not bath them.'

Nancy said, 'This is on, is it? You're not playing?'

'It's on.'

The baby had got hold of a tea-cup left on the arm of the sofa. It fell with a clatter to the floor and broke. 'I'll smack you,' snapped Nancy. The little face studied her for a moment, then suffused a deep red. The lower lip jutted.

Lungs drew breath ready to bellow.

'You shouldn't have left it there,' said Dell. But the incident jerked Nancy into action. By six o'clock a battered brown suitcase, a grip, and a basket of odds and ends crowned by a pink pot stood near the door. 'You'll need the pushchair too,' said Dell. 'Never mind clearing up, I'll do that. Now I'm going to disappear the moment he comes. Pretend I'm not here. Put the lights out. Look as if you're locking up. And keep still a minute, you.' The last was to the baby. Dell was struggling to persuade short, wilful arms into the sleeves of a zippered pram suit already half a size too small. Tony was already enveloped in a little duffle coat, his thin face cowled in its hood, his thin legs projecting below like stalks. He said, continually, insistently, 'Are we going in our car, Dad, or in another car? How many horsepowers is it? Will we be back for the bonfire?' He only stopped to cough; Dell glanced up briefly, troubled by the dark shadowy eyes in the pale face.

Five minutes before the quarter-hour Dell retreated upstairs. From the darkness of Tony's bedroom he could just see the lights of cars on the road. Two sets went past, then a third slowed and the beams swept round and for a moment shone into his eyes as the car lurched slowly into the bridle path. The beams dipped and rose again with the bumps. He remembered something suddenly and called to Nancy, 'Hey, did a fat photographer with a mealy head turn up?'

Nancy sounded puzzled. 'Not unless it was when I was out at the shops. I wrapped up Tony well and took him along with the baby. He wanted to buy another firework and it seemed a bit milder —'

'All right, all right. It was probably as well. I only hope he doesn't come now. There's something coming, anyway.'

Backing away from the window he heard the car stop and begin a laborious reversing manoeuvre. Then came a knock at the door, surprisingly loud, and the baby starting to cry at the unexpectedness of it; Nancy's voice, reassuring; the sound of her unlatching and opening the door, murmured exchanges. Tony's monotonous piping floated up clearly, 'Where's Dad, isn't Dad coming?' and Nancy's reply, which Dell guessed rather than heard, 'You'll see your Dad in a minute.' There was the repeated slamming of doors, more to-ing and fro-ing, the creak of the stair and Nancy's cool, acceptant whisper, 'We're off now, love. See you soon.'

Dell watched the red tail lights creep away towards the road and jerked into action. Downstairs a low fire afforded a minimal flickering light. Dell checked the curtains and re-lit one of the oil lamps before setting off on a careful sweep of the room, throwing toys, books, papers, into some semblance of order; into the middle of the floor went a cherished teddy bear that the baby might want, a ten-year-old AA guidebook that Dell had bought for a penny at a jumble sale, anything else to be taken on the journeys ahead. Upstairs, using the torch to avoid too much light, he bundled his two best shirts, a thick pullover, change of underclothes, flannel pyjamas and a pair of slippers into the limp khaki hold-all he found, thick with dust, on top of the wardrobe where it had lain for three years. He checked on what Nancy had taken of her own: it seemed enough, except for the old white sweater which had been his until it shrank and which she would sometimes wear in the depths of winter.

Resting the torch on the bed he changed quickly into his best tweed jacket and twill trousers and hunted in the depths of the wardrobe for the thick navy-blue donkey jacket he'd bought seven years before from a Liverpool-Irish labourer. The contractor's name was still stencilled faintly on the back. Finally he raided the beds, the baby's cot and Tony's room for the half dozen warmest blankets and rolled them into one bundle.

Downstairs again, he added the hold-all to the pile in the middle of the floor, felt his chin and veered into the kitchen to put the kettle on for a shave. He darted back into the living room to poke the dying fire back into life and add some pieces of wood. From the shed he recovered the old tin box and opening it in the light of the single oil-lamp went through the contents. The useless passport went into the grate, followed by some newspaper cuttings, ochre-coloured from age and damp. A bundle of letters tied with a now colourless ribbon Dell weighed briefly in his hand, then added to the smouldering fire. He put aside a miniature slide-rule in a leather case, a Kodak wallet containing half a dozen snapshots, a pair of spectacles in a case, lastly a little cotton bag from which he tipped, and counted, seventeen gold sovereigns. He'd started buying them one at a time as part of the standard escape plan which had been so neglected lately. He stood up and prised off the back of the mantel clock that never went. A tight bundle of notes fell out. Dell stuffed them uncounted into the cotton bag with the gold coins; he knew that there was exactly forty-two pounds.

It was five to seven. In the kitchen the kettle was whistling. Dell peeled off his pullover and shirt and began to lather his face.

Suddenly there was a hammering at the front door.

Dell instinctively spun round on his heel, then froze. He waited, holding his breath, razor in hand, willing the sound not to repeat itself.

It came again, more loudly.

Then there was the squeak of the latch being tried.

With a crack the door opened and a figure struggled with the hanging blanket. A second later the great speckled face of Mealy-head the Photographer was glaring into the room. At first he didn't see Dell.

'I say, anyone at home,' he called. 'Anyone there?'

Dell said, 'Oh, it's you, is it? What do you want?' He went over and stood in the doorway into the living-room.

'Just want to get those pix we were discussing earlier. You know, packing up and so on.' His eyes strayed to the hold-all and the little pile of goods on the floor.

'That was the afternoon. It's evening now. You're too late.'

'Now, just a minute, just a minute!' Mealy-head's voice switched to practised truculence. 'I came this afternoon, just as I said. And nobody in! Not a dickey-bird. Who's fault's that? Not mine!'

'They were out shopping I expect. You could have come back a little later.'

'We-ell, the office sent me off to London Airport to get old Philip arriving, for the Daily. Couldn't help it, mate. Then I had to take the stuff in and drive all the flippin' way out here again. I said we could have done the job tomorrow but they said they wanted one of your good wife bathing the kids, like Hunter described. Where are they, gone to bed already? I won't be long, promise.'

'I'm not disturbing them now,' said Dell. 'You'd better go.'

'Five minutes, honest.' He unslung his camera and rummaged in a leather grip for extras.

Dell went back to the sink and began shaving quickly, firmly. 'Look, would you kindly go. You're not seeing anyone tonight. You had your chance. Now please go.'

'Now listen, mate, I believe you're on the payroll in a manner of speaking. That wasn't a five-bob postal order I brought out this morning for you. I'm tired. I've had a long day.' He looked down at his feet. 'I've got my shoes plastered in mud and my lungs full of a terrible stink marching up this lane in the dark because I wasn't going to risk the car again, not in the dark. All I'm asking is five minutes with the wife and the kids. I'll tell you what — you needn't even get the kids up. I'll forget the bath. We'll make do with Mum telling them a story while they're tucked up in bed.'

Dell stretched his upper lip down to attack the last patch of stubble. 'I'm sorry, you can't.'

'Very well, then,' — in minatory tones — 'I'll have to have a word with the office. Do you know what I'll tell them? I'll tell them I think the family has skipped already, and that by the looks of things you're about to do the same. I think they'd be interested. I thought it was tomorrow Bob Hunter said he was taking you.'

Dell wiped his face with the roller towel on the back of the kitchen door. He walked back into the living room, collecting his shirt on the way. Mealy-head was coupling an electronic flash to his camera. There was a faint drone as he switched on the power pack slung at his side. He said, 'Well I might as well get one of you at home while I'm about it —'

Dell kicked out. His shoe missed the camera and caught the flash gear. The bang of the impact was followed by a thud and the rattle of breaking glass as the whole apparatus hit the ground. Dell's toe, where the nail grew in, started to hurt with a steady, fierce, pain.

Mealy-head bent and scooped up the gear. The flash reflector was crumpled and the little glass bulb shattered. The camera looked all right to Dell's eye but there was an ominous tinkling of glass from somewhere inside the reflex hood.

'Very well,' said Mealy-head. He was breathing heavily, either from affront or the exertion of bending. 'Ve-ry well. So that's how it is, is it?'

Dell banged the heel of his shoe on the floor in an effort to relieve pressure on his toe. He discovered that he was breathing heavily, too. 'Yes, that's just how it is,' he said lamely.

'You've put your foot in it properly now, mate. You don't get away with that sort of lark. That's assault.'

'And you're trespassing.'

'Oh no, I'm not. You invited me here. And I'll remind you I've your note in my pocket to prove it. Now I think you'd better come along with me to the nearest police station.'

Dell shook his head. He tapped his heel again. 'Another time perhaps.'

Mealy-head's ponderous calm vanished. His face went red. 'Listen, these cameras are our property, you know. They don't belong to the firm. I'm not having any lousy little tuppeny-ha-penny traitor bashing up my gear!'

Dell hopped up and down on his good foot. It was cold with the door open, and he with no shirt on. 'I kick better with my left foot,' he said warningly.

'Now listen,' said Mealy-head. But he took a pace backwards. Dell advanced one. Mealy-head thrust his camera elaborately behind him, as if to protect it with his own body. He still took another backward step. Dell got his right hand on to the door and his left on to the hanging blanket, jerking it aside. Mealy-head said, 'Watch it, just watch it, mate,' and abruptly backed out and was gone.

Dell banged the door after him, stood stock still for a moment in thought, then launched himself into desperate action. In the kitchen he tipped a pint of milk into a saucepan and put it on the gas, hunted for the thermos flask, found it, washed it out. Somewhere else on the shelves was the old lunch box he'd carried when he worked in the bus depot. He located it, rubbed the inside out with a tea-towel, put in a packet of biscuits, all the apples he could find, half a pound of cheese, a little knife with a red handle.

There wasn't time to load the car properly. Dell hooked up the rear flap and made three, four, five journeys between house and shed, first with the roll of blankets, then the hold-all, then the other oddments. From the kitchen came the hiss and splutter and cloying smell of milk boiling over. He hurried through, turned out the gas, poured the milk into the thermos flask and on the impulse added the inch of whisky left in the bottom of Hunter's bottle. It remained only to bolt and lock the front door, break up the last pieces of coal and charred paper in the fireplace, extinguish the oil lamps. He stood in the silent darkness for a moment. He became aware of the ticking of the alarm clock upstairs, faint but distinct, and started to make a move towards it; then remembered Nancy's little radio in the kitchen and collected that instead. Bumping down the bridle path without lights he swore and murmured, 'Tony's fireworks!' His foot eased momentarily on the accelerator. Then he pressed it again.

The clock in the clock tower by Maidenhead Station indicated 8.15 as Dell turned the car into the forecourt. Nancy appeared at once. She was holding the baby, Tony followed lugging the basket. 'Where were you?' she wanted to know. 'We've been waiting and it's cold and Tony only up today the first time. You might have been here on time for —'

'Something happened,' snapped Dell. 'Tell you in a minute. Get in quickly.'

As they drove out of the forecourt Tony said, 'Where we going? Are we going to Ireland. Are we going on a train?'

'Right now,' said Nancy. 'We're not going anywhere. We're going home to bed, double-quick.'

'I'm afraid we're not,' said Dell apologetically.

'And I'm afraid we are! What are you thinking of?'

'I told you. Something happened. That damned photographer turned up, the one that should have been here this afternoon.'

'Well?'

'He got nasty. I happened to break his camera, and he went off threatening to get the police, and to telephone his wretched office. Either way, it could stop us leaving tomorrow. So the only thing is to go now.'

'You mean … right away, for good? Oh no, no!'

'There's no alternative.'

'But I must clear up. I can't just leave the house like it was … there's things we need…'

'I cleared up,' said Dell patiently. 'I got everything we need — at least, everything we've room for.' He turned out of the main street into the back road to Cookham.

Nancy looked out of the window. 'This is the way home, isn't it? It's one of the ways home. You've been kidding us.'

'I wish I had.'

'Oh God, what's to become of us?' She started to sniff.

Dell hissed, 'Please don't. You'll set Tony off.' He heard the click of the fastener of her bag as she looked for a handkerchief. He reached out a hand and held hers for a second. Later there was the scratch of a match and the flicker of its flame. Out of the corner of his eye Dell could see her profile illumined as she drew on her cigarette. When she was sad was the only time she could be called beautiful. He became aware again of Tony, leaning forward from the rear seat. 'Aren't there any lights inside? Can't we have lights?'

'You can't have lights inside a car while you're going along. The driver wouldn't be able to see out properly.'

'You have lights in buses, don't you?'

'That's different,' said Dell, and then, making an effort, 'Usually he has a little blind he pulls down, so that his cab stays in the dark. Or in some buses I remember when I was going to school the inside lights were blue and the window between the driver and the passengers was yellow. Blue light doesn't go through yellow glass.'

'Why doesn't it?'

'Well, it just doesn't.' He corrected himself again. 'It's as if the yellow glass subtracted the light from the blue bulbs. I suppose it must have been because of the Blackout.'

'What's Blackout?'

'It was when we were fighting other countries, and all the lights in the houses and streets and everywhere had to be covered up so that the other countries' aeroplanes wouldn't know when they were over the big towns.' To change the subject he added hurriedly, 'The light in this car is very simple.' He fumbled round the primitive instrumentation and found the switch. A tiny lamp above the windscreen emitted a narrow ray of light on to the speedometer below. Dell twisted the housing and light spilled into the cabin through a slot. Tony gazed at it in wonder.

Nancy was looking out of the window. 'Are we going to pass home?'

'Not quite.'

'Well, can we?'

'Safer not to.'

'I forgot to leave the milk money.'

'That would mean going right back.'

'No, I've got it all ready. I was going to leave it on the way home anyway.' She leaned close to him and whispered, 'Did you remember Tony's fireworks? He was asking about them.'

Dell didn't reply, but took the fork that would lead them past the end of the bridle-path, which was as far as the milkman would venture in his electric float. Nancy was rummaging in the basket at her feet for the cocoa tin which she left out every Friday with the money and milk-tokens inside. Dell pushed the gearstick forward into second to drive slowly past the end of the path, searching for any signs of life, ready to accelerate away. There was nothing.

He braked.

'Give it to me. I'll leave it.' He ran across the road. There was an old wooden post which had survived from the days when the path had been gated. Dell put the tin at its foot as he had done a hundred times before. He looked down the path but in the darkness the cottage was invisible. Then something approaching made him look back at the road. Wobbling towards him was the single, low-placed light of a cyclist. Dell hurried back to the car and pulled away as quietly as he could. As they passed the cycle he kept his head averted but watched the stately figure carefully in his rear mirror. It seemed to be dismounting.

'The village cop,' he whispered to Nancy. 'I hope he didn't notice too much. Now, what's the matter?'

But Nancy wasn't crying. She was laughing. 'A flit,' she said. 'We've flitted. My Mum and Dad were always talking about the times they had to do it, when we kids were little. When they were about six weeks behind with the rent and the electricity was going to be turned off they'd load all their gear on a handcart and pile the pram with pots and pans and flit. Now I know what it was like. Only we've got a car. Our car, eh?' she touched Dell on the sleeve. 'Hey, tell us about this photographer chap. What did you do to him?'

'I kicked him in the camera! He was a big fat man with a big red face that looked as if it had been dipped in a bran tub, it was a real mealy-head, and he spoke like this, 'Now watch it, mate, I'm telling you, watch it!" Dell mimicked exaggeratedly.

Tony giggled, not really understanding anything but catching the change of mood in the front seats. Dell told the story with discreet embroidery. When he'd finished Nancy clapped her hands as best she could and improvised a chorus for Tony and her to sing, and the baby to laugh at:

We kicked him in the camera,
We kicked him in the camera,
We kicked him in the cam-er-a,
Silly old Mealy-head.

It lasted all the way through Beaconsfield and half-way to Amersham as Dell drove steadily north.

Under a street lamp in a side-road they pulled out most of the stuff that Dell had thrown into the back and repacked it. Nancy changed the baby, who'd started to grizzle, and gave both children drinks of hot milk from the thermos. She sniffed it suspiciously.

'Did you put something in?'

'The last drop of that whisky. Won't do any harm, may even help them to sleep.'

Dell fiddled with the homemade rear seats and managed to remove one of them. 'We won't really need it again,' he said, and dropped it carefully over the front hedge of a house called 'The Gables'. In the space it left there was room to bed down both the baby and Tony, head to tail, wrapped in blankets. A bundle of nappies served as a pillow for the baby, another nappy, spread over a rolled coat, for Tony.

As they turned back on to the main road Nancy shivered and said, 'Will they be warm enough?'

'There's a heater of sorts,' Dell slowed the car and groped for the lever amid the oily felt that backed the engine bulkhead. 'There's one on your side, too. A little lever. Pull it across.'

'I can feel it already, on my legs,' she said. 'Nice and warm. How far we going tonight? Where do we stay?'

'Not sure; a bit further yet.'

'I'm hungry. Did you remember any food?'

'A bit. It's in the old lunch-box.'

They ate sweet biscuits and cheese and apples, in no particular order, Nancy doing the cutting and spreading and peeling and keeping Dell supplied. They stopped once to study the map. In Hemel Hempstead new town Nancy gazed at the clean patterns of glass and brick, the trees, the wide, climbing roads. They passed a white new church. People were coming away or standing talking at the porch while above them a tall window, almost the whole width of the wall, glowed sea-green and mysterious from the illumination within.

She said, 'It looks like a new world.'

'They're supposed to be dull, or something, new towns.'

'I'd chance it.'

Dell said, 'You're right. If only the whole country were like this … I mean, if things could be planned and built and done to some ideal, not just to make money or keep some bloody old tradition alive … well for one thing we wouldn't be here in this tin-can vehicle with nowhere to go on a cold night.'

Nancy lit a cigarette. 'Why did you do what you did, that time ago? You never really told me.'

'If I'd known myself I might have done. I was trying to sort something out for Hunter. It didn't make much sense.'

She was frowning with concentration. 'But you don't understand, you don't begin to understand. You didn't even *try* with me. It's as if all that time was nothing to do with me, as if it belonged to someone else.' She picked a fragment of cigarette paper from her lip. 'I sometimes wonder if you were married to some woman before me...'

Dell said, 'No, I wasn't married. There was a girl, that's all. By the way, I forgot.' He reached in the glove compartment. 'I brought your little radio. We can have some music.' They passed through Luton, Hitchin and the trim gravelly outskirts of Letchworth. The engine whirred away smoothly, only the thud of the worn-out suspension if they hit a pothole began to worry Dell. The patching-up Stephen had performed wouldn't last very long. They drove through Baldock and a deserted Royston and into Cambridge as the caramel tones of the Light Programme announcer began to break the news that they would be closing down in a minute. As Trumpington Street gave way to King's Parade a clock began to chime midnight. Dell pulled up just before the cobbled forecourt to King's. One by one clocks all over the town joined in to make a formless melody.

'The students have until the last stroke to get in,' Dell told Nancy. 'One of the clocks strikes thirteen so that's an extra second, I suppose.' As they watched, a solitary figure, short black gown fluttering over his overcoat, crossed the road and stood jiffling with impatience by the bell-push. A door in the big gates opened and he stepped inside. 'Just made it, I should think.'

Nancy said, 'Is this where you were?'

'Right here. In this college.'

Nancy craned her head to one side to look at the alien rounded domes of the Screen and beyond them the twelve pinnacles of the chapel, ghostly white against a night sky that seemed a bit clearer than it had been further south. She tugged and pushed at the window, and unable to move it, opened the whole door instead. She shivered and shut it again.

'A cold wind.'

'I know. It used to seem colder and rawer than any other place I'd ever been. I remember once running back to get in by midnight, just like the one we saw a minute ago. I'd had a few drinks and I was bursting to go to the lavatory — you know how it's worse when it's cold. I rang the bell and I was dancing up and down waiting for them to answer. I daren't go away for fear of being late.'

'What happened?'

'I just got inside and was running through the court when I peed myself. It must have been the first time since I'd been a little boy. It was a funny feeling.'

She looked at him fondly. 'There you are, you see — I know a bit more about you. I never knew anything like that about you before.'

Dell laughed. 'Hardly very illuminating.' He started the motor again. 'Don't know what we're doing standing here, though.'

Past King's, Clare, Caius, Trinity and St. John, Dell steered his way carefully through an unfamiliar tangle of one-way streets, heading for a terrace of tall Victorian houses near the Park. He stopped outside the last one. It was in darkness but he could pick out the brass plate on the door.

'It's still there anyway!' he muttered; then to Nancy, 'Well, this is as far as we go tonight. I suppose we'd better find a hotel.'

'A *hotel*! I've never stayed in one. I wouldn't know what to do.'

'It's that or nothing at this time of night.'

'I thought you were just going on and on.' She looked round at the sleeping children. 'It seems a pity to disturb the nips.'

Dell considered, 'I suppose we could sit it out in the car. Not here, though.' He drove on, across the Newmarket Road and over the common. 'It's called Midsummer Common,' he said.

'B-rr-r. I wish it was.'

'It always used to remind me of a poem, the beginning of a play, actually. I don't know why; just the word *summer* I suppose.' He quoted falteringly:

The Summer holds: upon its glittering lake
Lie Europe and the Islands: many rivers
Wrinkling its surface like a ploughman's palm...

He flashed the headlights, dip-full, full-dip, dip-full, to turn on to the Kings Lynn road. 'I forgot how it went on. Auden, Isherwood, McNeice, people like that — they were our heroes when I was here. And earlier. We used to read them at school instead of the things we were supposed to read. They were always thin books with big flowing letters on the dustcover. You had to hide them from the masters because they were supposed to be too Left for respectable grammar school boys. It seemed so simple then, to us, anyway. Left was right and Right was wrong. You had a picture of greedy capitalists and arms manufacturers — you know, I'd quite forgotten: I saw a ballet here in Cambridge when I was up. The Provost took all the freshmen. He said, 'I don't like ballet all that thumping about,' but they were lucky to get anything at the theatre at all in wartime. Anyway, it was modern, highly political allegorical outfit and one of the ballets was all about a disarmament conference and blow me there were all the bogeymen just as

I'd imagined them, bald dictator and frock-coated arms king and everyone … '

Nancy said, 'Yeah,' uncomprehendingly.

Dell was looking for somewhere to pull off the road. He added, 'And that was about the only time I went out in the whole two years. I had to work too hard.'

'Except the time you wet yourself.'

'Except the time I wet myself.'

Dell turned off into a side road and then off that on to the grass verge under a big swaying elm. He twisted in his seat and rummaged in the back.

'Careful,' said Nancy suddenly whispering. 'What do you want?'

'Bit of sacking or something.' He found a square of the rubber floor matting which came away. 'This'll do. Just to muffle the air intake.'

'Are you going to leave the engine going?'

'Crikey, yes. We'd freeze. This should make it run a bit hotter.' He slipped out and wedged the corners of the rubber into the slotted bonnet front. It was cold all right, a damp raw cold. He frowned at the thought of Tony having to spend the night with only the protection of a flimsy car body and the heat of two little idling cylinders.

Inside Nancy had spread out the last two blankets over the front seat. The car swayed and creaked as they settled themselves. Dell let himself slump in his seat so that he leaned against Nancy at his side. He stretched his legs as far as they'd go between the pedals, and wrapped the blanket ends around him to meet Nancy's. For the moment, anyway, it was comfortable. On his leg he could feel the warm air wafted through from the engine. He said, 'Is there any of that milk left?'

'Should be.' She reached down and after a moment handed him the thermos cup. The milk was still quite hot and the whisky gave it a comforting body.

'You have some. It seems to have laid the kids out all right.'

She tried. 'Ugh. Don't like the taste.'

'Go on, drink it. It'll help you to sleep.'

Presently he heard her screw the cup back on the flask, then she was snuggling against him, drawing the blankets tight around them both. Her hair brushed the side of his face. She said, 'If you'd told me twenty-four hours ago where we'd be now I'd never have believed you.'

'Mmm,' said Dell.

'Where'll we be in another twenty-four?'

'God knows.'

'But it'll be all right, won't it?'

'It'll be all right.'

Dell reached out to rub the windscreen which was misting over. But it wasn't mist inside. It was frost outside that blurred the outline of the swaying elm.

CHAPTER 4: FRIDAY

Dell lost count of how many times he woke, cramped and chilled, to shift his position and pull the blankets tighter. He found that covering his head completely helped him to doze. Once he dreamed he was back aboard a Transport Command Dakota descending through the clouds, listening anxiously to the muffled note of the motors, only to surface again and slowly identify the sound as the rhythm of the car engine. He longed to stretch out, to lie down. Nancy was obviously no happier.

Around 4 a.m. Tony began to cough, at first in his sleep, then gradually forced into wakefulness. Nancy swivelled in her seat, sat up and gave him the last of the hot milk. After a while he slept again.

The first grey light of day brought some dispirited birdsong from the sheltering tree and others near it. The baby woke, with a sighing and stretching and a little fart. At first she only chattered to herself. Later she grew restless, missing the familiar bars of her cot and surrounding toys. Nancy found a teddy bear in the basket and put it in reach.

'Ted-dy, ted-dy,' said the baby, pleased. It would distract her for ten minutes with luck.

The hour from six to seven dragged by. They switched the wireless on, caught the end of a news summary and listened to some band sleep-walking its way through a procession of middle-weight blues.

'How do they make every one sound the same?' asked Dell. He was cold. His unshaven beard was sore and scratchy. His teeth were coated and his gums ached. The air in the car was awful.

'I think the baby's smelly,' said Nancy.

Dell went for a walk while she was changed, shivering in the outside cold. He pulled the rubber square from the radiator grille and used it to wipe down the smeary windscreen.

He kicked the tires. They seemed all right. Inside again the stench was familiar but still enough to make his stomach contract.

'What shall I do with the nappy?' asked Nancy.

'Sling it,' said Dell anti-socially.

'But I'll run out at that rate.'

'We'll have to get some of those paper pad things instead. It may be days before you get a chance to wash anything. How's Tony?'

Nancy made a resigned face. 'Well, he's quite cheery.'

'Are we going more in the car, Daddy? Where we going in the car?' He lengthened the word 'car' to give it an overriding importance. But he looked pale and shadowy under the eyes.

'Oh, yes, a bit further,' said Dell. 'Hadn't you better have a little walk outside. Have a look at a tree?'

When he judged there was a reasonable chance of finding somewhere open, he rubbed the inside of the windscreen and revved the engine a moment and turned to drive back the way they'd come. As the little car lurched off the verge the warning light blinked a reminder that they'd soon need more petrol.

Negotiating the tangle of one-way streets in the town centre again Dell said, 'There used to be a Joe Lyon's somewhere round Petty Cury — down there in fact if it wasn't a No Entry. Sometimes I'd go out for breakfast on a Saturday morning, just for a change, big treat, though what there can have been to eat, in the middle of the war, I can't think. All I can remember is the glass of orange juice to start with, straight out of the bottle. I used to think that was gracious living.'

Nancy said, 'We can't go anywhere like this. We look like gypsies.'

'I know where we can clean up.'

Dell followed signs to a car park. It turned out to be off a back street between the Market Square and Corpus Christi. He led the way back to the square on foot and they dived down their respective flights of steps; Nancy holding the baby, into the Ladies; Dell and Tony into the Gents. Dell stripped off his jacket and shirt and lathered his face. Tony paddled his hands listlessly in the adjacent basin. His nose only just cleared the rim.

'Tony, for heaven's sake take off your duffle coat. You can't wash properly with your face in a hood!'

Tony stared back in dismay.

'It's all right,' said Dell hastily. 'I didn't mean to bark at you. You know, *wuff-wuff*, like the dogs go.' He bent down and undid the toggles and eased the duffle coat off Tony's shoulders. 'One little arm,' he said, reverting to the patter they'd used years earlier. '*Another* little arm. Now your pullover, *off* it comes!'

'I want Mummy to wash me.'

'Yes, well, Mummy's not allowed in here, you see. She's with the baby in another place just like this, only for ladies!'

They emerged in the end, reasonably presentable. The sleep was out of Tony's eyes and his hair was combed and the hood of the duffle coat allowed to fall back. Nancy was waiting for them, the baby clutching a biscuit and glowing with wellbeing.

'If I hadn't given her something she'd have gone crazy.'

Dell bought a paper and they filed into the cafeteria, deserted still except for two busmen and an R.A.F. corporal who looked as if he'd been out all night. The smells of tea and bacon and toast were rich in promise. The baby's eyes were wide in wonder, her head swivelling round and back again to take in the colour and chrome and array of red-topped tables. Even Tony was on tip-toes, insistent on piloting his own tray along the self-service counter.

After orange juice (for old times' sake), porridge, bacon and eggs, with a second helping of tea before him, Dell felt ready to look at the paper. Something led his eye to the item almost at once. Even so, he saw it for a fraction of a second without comprehending. Instinctively he glanced up at Nancy, folding the paper away from her. She was occupied with the baby. He took another, longer, unbelieving look.

The paper was one of the solid, more sober dailies. The report was short and wary. It was headed MISSING SCIENTIST REPORTED and underneath, Link with Spy Case. The text said that according to an unconfirmed report John Bristow, who would now be 37 and who had vanished at the time of the Longbow security investigation in 1954, had been working under an assumed name in a home counties car assembly depot. A Home Office spokesman declined to comment on whether his department had any knowledge of the report. He was unable to say whether Bristow, if he did turn up, would face any charges. The report ended with a brief resumé of the original case, which had culminated with the suicide of Dr. Roy Cliente in an hotel room in Milan. The Longbow project had been abandoned in 1958.

Dell left the family finishing breakfast and hurried out into the town. In Sidney Street the shops were opening up with a rattle of locks and iron night-gates. The first undergraduates wobbled past on old bikes or hurried along Downing Street bound for the nine o'clock start at the engineering labs. Dell walked briskly; the morning air was refreshing on his face where he'd shaved.

In the terrace near the park he stopped to tie his shoelace and take a quick look round. There was no one much about. He went up to the house with the brass plate. It was engraved Collegiate Correspondence College, the letters worn and smooth. Above it a new, larger, plastic sign announced Collegiate School of English. Dell turned the massive door knob and stepped into the hall. The door into a front office stood open, showing it empty of life, the typewriters hooded, the electric sign that said enquiries unlit. But a G.P.O. mailbag had been roughly tipped out over the lino'd floor, making a ragged pile of uniform-sized manila envelopes each bearing a printed label.

There was a staircase straight ahead. Dell started up it, not too fast, making plenty of noise. From inside a half open door on the first landing a voice called with a trace of foreign accent, 'Is that you, Miss James?'

Dell stopped and said, 'No, I'm afraid it's not.'

Feet thudded to the door. Their owner poked his head round. 'Who is that? There is no one here yet. The school does not open until nine-thirty. In any case —'

Dell said, 'Good morning, Principal. I couldn't be sure you were still here. I'm glad you are.'

The Principal peered down at him. He said, 'I cannot see you. Who is it?' He pulled his spectacles down to the end of his nose and tried looking over them.

'You probably wouldn't remember the name,' said Dell. 'I met you through Roy Cliente and did some marking in wave mechanics for you —'

'*Bristow*! Why have you come here? This morning of all mornings? Please leave at once, before the staff arrive.'

'It's all right. It's not nine yet.' Dell resumed his ascent.

The Principal peered at him over his glasses. 'You are really Bristow?' he said questioningly. 'Yes, yes, I see it now. Without the beard it is not obvious. Did anyone see you enter this house?' He backed slowly into the room from which he had emerged. He was holding some letters and a postcard in his hand.

'No one. I was careful. I remembered how you liked to arrive early to sift through the post.'

'You had better come in,' said the Principal belatedly. On his desk was a newspaper, a different one from Dell's. He folded it to present one small facet and thrust it at Dell. 'You saw this? You have certainly chosen a fine morning to come and visit!'

'Is it in all the papers?'

'I imagine so. They appear to be prompted by something they have seen in one of their more sensational fellows, which one I do not yet know —'

'Well, that's why I'm here,' said Dell. 'Or to be more exact, why *we're* here. I've a wife and two kids in the town.'

'What do you want?'

'To get away. You once said you could get me a job on the other side.'

'Impossible!'

Dell said, 'You're doing quite nicely by the looks of things. English classes for foreigners — that's something new. Do you hold them here? I'd like to stay and see —'

'Bristow, what do you want of me?'

'What I said. You once told me —'

'Will you promise to go at once if I do help you?'

'I'll be out of Cambridge before your school opens.'

'Very well. You asked about a post abroad? I may have mentioned the possibility once, but that was seven years ago or more. They have caught up since then. You, on the contrary, have marked time — even lost ground.' His eyes dropped pointedly. 'Your hands are hardly the hands of a professional man.'

'I've been working in a garage. Professional men need qualifications. Qualifications predispose identification. That's the thing I don't have.'

The Principal pursed his lips. 'Have you thought of somewhere else in the West? After all there is generally no extradition in cases of espionage … it would not be difficult to establish a political motive for anything you may have done…'

'You don't get people like Philips or Ducretet-Thomson employing security suspects, not if they want to keep their NATO contracts. It has to be Russia or nothing.'

'*Russia!*' The Principal raised his eyebrows. 'I don't think you understand…' His voice tailed off. 'All I can offer you is an introduction to a certain other country. But first you must escape from this one. Have you some means of that?'

'I've an idea, that's all.'

'I'm sorry I cannot be of assistance. If, however, you can get to the Netherlands … is that possible?'

'As possible as anywhere.'

The Principal looked at him thoughtfully. His voice became brisk. 'Very well. I can put you in touch with someone. Whether he can do anything for you is another matter … how old are the children?'

'The boy's six, the girl's only one.'

The Principal frowned. 'It may not be easy … still, you can cross that bridge when you come to it. Now, you know the red light district in Amsterdam?'

'No.'

'Well, it is not difficult to find; a short way from the railway station. Go in the early evening, that is best. The girls are in little boutiques, so to speak. They sit in the window combing their hair or sitting by a table lamp with a red shade and it all looks very inviting. You must, however, control yourself' — he smirked — 'and find a narrow alley called the Hoofsteg. Remember that, don't write it down, Hoof like a horse's hoof. There is only one girl in the Hoofsteg. If she is occupied' — again the smirk — 'the curtains will be drawn. You must be patient and take a walk round the block and perhaps drink a glass of beer. If the girl is free, go in and pretend you wish to avail yourself of her services — as indeed you may like to. I understand the young lady is both personable and cleanly.' He cocked his head on one side, 'But sooner or later, Bristow, you must declare yourself and I will tell you how. You promise you will make no notes, only trust your memory?'

Dell nodded.

The Principal began to usher him towards the stairs. 'You must say you are from the Diner's Club.' He permitted himself a giggle. 'It's a little joke against the Americans we couldn't resist. I would like to see their faces! Anyway, you say this and ask if you can have services on credit. The girl will say, No, of course not, and you say, Then I wish to see Mr. East. It should be Mynheer Oost really, but the girl will accept the anglicisation. She'll show you into a small room at the back and there you must wait until East, or Oost, comes. There are compensations, I believe — quite a good view of whatever may be going on in the other room, if you can find the peephole.'

Dell scowled. 'You can skip the titillation,' he said.

The Principal hung his head in mock regret. 'I was forgetting. You're a family man now. Anyway, that's it. You wait for this man and he will do what he can do.' They were going down the staircase now. The Principal rested, his hand lightly on Dell's shoulder. 'You must appreciate, that it is not a high-powered organisation. We no longer belong on that plane, neither of us. Think of it just as a form of — workers' travel agency which perhaps can assist your passage.'

'Passage where, Principal?' The Principal spread his hand deprecatingly. 'Ah, I can't deceive you. It would be the German Democratic Republic. I would like to offer you the hope of something better, but honestly no other country would be in need of your — er — somewhat suspended talents.' He reached for the watch again. 'Now I *must* ask you to excuse me. Quite apart from anything else staff will be arriving...' He called after Dell, 'I hope you get on all right. I'm sure you will.'

They were waiting for him in the car park, the baby sitting on a pot between Nancy's feet. Tony deep in Dell's paper. He could read the headlines and sometimes the captions. He said, 'What's adult-ry mean, Daddy?'

'Never mind now,' said Dell shortly, fumbling for the starter.

'You should tell him,' said Nancy reproachfully. 'Tell him something. It's not right to shut them up when they ask questions like that.'

'For God's sake, we're on the run and all you can think about is how to bring up the kids.' He raced the motor to warm it. There was a policeman across the street from the exit of the park, huge and majestic and not twenty yards away. Dell pulled the gear-shift out into first and jerked forward.

'Just a minute!' yelled Nancy. 'You'll have this all over the floor. Can't you see she's on the pot?'

'Can't help that,' said Dell. He turned sharply right to head the way they'd come in. The drive wheels fought in the hard lock and the car shuddered. Nancy swore. The policeman stepped ponderously off the kerb and raised a hand like a plank. Dell braked and shoved up his window flap. The policeman walked slowly round the nose of the car, furrowing his brow. He stooped and lowered a pink, scraped jowl level with Dell's face, pushed his chin strap clear of his mouth with a jerk of his lower jaw and said. 'Excuse me, sir, but is your car all right?'

'What do you mean?'

'What do I mean? I mean the front wheels. Turning round that corner then they was leaning all ways. I've never seen anything like it.' He'd dropped the 'sir' already.

Dell said, 'They're meant to. They do that. It's the suspension.'

'I've never seen it before.'

'Well, maybe you haven't seen this make of car before. There aren't many of them in England. I can assure you it's perfectly safe.'

The policeman chewed his chin strap. He stood back and looked at the wheels again. He reached out a massive arm and the suspension creaked as he rocked the car. Then the pink jowl reappeared and a pair of cold blue eyes surveyed the interior. He said, 'Are you going far?'

Dell said, 'No, not far. Bury St. Edmunds.'

'Well, you're going the wrong way then.'

'It's these one way streets,' said Dell hurriedly. 'I got mixed up. I can still turn right up at the traffic lights, can't I?'

'All right then,' said the policeman. He stood back again. Dell said, 'Thank you' — he didn't know what for — and got away again, more smoothly this time. In the rear-view mirror he could see the policeman standing fixedly in the middle of the street, watching them.

'Blinking cheek,' said Nancy. 'What does he know about cars, eh?' She made it bright and cheerful, so as not to alarm Tony. Dell shivered; a trickle of cold sweat coasted down under his armpit. At the traffic lights he turned left on to the Huntingdon road. When they were clear of the town he slowed. Nancy lifted the baby off the pot.

'There's a good girl. We've got something from you this time.' To nobody in particular she said, 'You know, we could almost start to train her.'

'Good,' said Dell absently. He was listening to the engine note, the thump of the suspension if they hit a hump. Neither sounded too bad. 'Let's have the wireless on.'

Nancy tracked down Housewives Choice, juggling the position of the little set to get the best reception and holding it up for Tony to hear in the back. He wriggled with delight at his favourites and groaned at the ones he didn't like. The sound came and went and sometimes got lost altogether. The baby pushed her legs down on the seat and jostled Dell and reached out a puffy pink hand for the gearshift. Dell said, 'No-o-o-oh' and pushed it away. Nancy lit a cigarette and the tension eased a bit more.

He said, 'Just when the whole trip was beginning to make sense that peasant had to put his great foot in it.'

'Never mind, love. He didn't do anything.'

'The trouble with the little car is that it's too conspicuous.'

'It's a smashing little car.'

'It's still too noticeable. I'll be glad when we get on to the A1. There's more traffic.'

At five to ten the disc programme finished and a hymn started up. 'Switch it off,' said Dell. 'I can't stand the little story they dish out afterwards. I thought there was some news mixed up with the Housewives Choice. What became of it?'

'It's at half-past,' said Nancy. 'We must have missed it. It's only a few bits, anyway.'

'What time's the next proper news.'

'One o'clock, I suppose.'

They reached Huntingdon soon after ten and the Great North Road a quarter of an hour later. Ten-forty and they passed through Stilton.

'Cheese,' said Dell. 'This is where the cheese comes from, very pongy.'

'Poo, poo, poo,' said Tony. 'Stinky old cheese. Poo.'

'Pu,' said the baby experimentally.

At Norman's Cross Dell pulled into the side and flicked through the AA book for the maps before forking right towards Peterborough. A clock indicated 11.15 as they skirted the town centre. Dell jabbed at the clutch to change down at a T-junction and there was a snapping noise and the pedal went dead under his foot. He swore.

Nancy started. 'What's up?'

'The clutch spring,' shouted Dell, 'the damned clutch spring.' He jiggled his foot back to see if the plates would drift together under their own weight. Nothing happened for what seemed like seconds. Someone behind rasped angrily on his horn. Then the drive connected but the laden car had lost too much speed and the engine faltered. Mouthing abuse at the horn blower Dell had to kick the unresisting pedal in again and grab first gear. Again the agonising wait; the other vehicle pulled out and passed, its driver scowling. As Dell glanced back the clutch finally connected and they shuddered forward.

'What's the *matter*?' hissed Nancy. Behind her, Tony's eyes were big with dismay.

Dell was looking for somewhere to draw up without being too conspicuous. The motor was whining away shrilly. He rammed the gearshift into second without using the clutch at all. The whining stopped and they picked up speed. He'd be able to get into third the same way. If they didn't have actually to stop dead, they might make it. At that moment he saw the sign Road Works Ahead and a line of cars halted at a red light.

'That's finished it,' he said. He swung the car to the side and braked viciously to a halt. In the mirror he caught a glimpse of Tony's face getting longer and longer. 'A sixpenny bloody spring, and I never thought of bringing a couple.'

Nancy whispered urgently, 'For God's sake, don't start him off…'

Dell shouted, 'Well, it's so bloody unnecessary. Just another twenty or thirty miles, that's all…' He rummaged wildly in the litter that Doggett had left in the deep tray down by the steering column. A pair of burned-out sparking plugs, a grease-caked rag, a stub of pencil, no little spring.

Tony was starting to whimper. Nancy glared at Dell and said over her shoulder, 'It's all right, love. It's nothing.'

Dell said, 'Maybe rubber bands would do it. Have you got any?'

'Me? — no, Tony might have one. Have you, Tony — a rubber band?' The sobbing stopped.

'One's no good,' said Dell curtly.

Nancy hissed, 'Haven't you any sense at all?'

Dell pulled himself together. He muttered, 'Sorry,' and to Tony, louder, 'Have you got one, Tony? We need it.'

The therapy worked. Tony said, 'I think so. Just a minit.' He sniffed and felt in his pockets. 'It's an orange one. They're the best.'

Dell tested its strength between his fingers. He said, 'Good old Tone, we'll see what happens.' Outside he found he was already in the fenlands. The grey sky seemed higher, the cold fen wind caught under the thin corrugated hood as he lifted it. The broken return spring had vanished, shooting off somewhere when the tension was released. Dell doubled the band, threaded it through the little anchor and wound it round the clutch arm as securely as he could. With luck it might last half a dozen gear changes.

He waited until the traffic was moving in the right direction and cautiously tried. The clutch was still soggy but responded more immediately. They got into third without trouble and out of the town. On a level straight bit he tried the overdrive fourth but the headwind was too strong; changing down again the band snapped. At Market Deeping they bought a packet of new ones from a stationer's shop. Dell harnessed six together. It took a while to fix them, and it was 12.30 by the time they got to Spalding.

They bought a pork pie and some bread rolls and two tins of infant food for the baby, and ate in the car, parked off in the asphalt yard at the side of a pub. Dell nursed a Guinness, Nancy said she'd give anything for a cup of tea. They turned the radio on and waited for the news. The weather forecast was of continuing cold weather, winds, the possibility of snow on high ground; there was a gale warning for two sea areas.

'Where's Dogger?' said Tony listlessly. The energy of earlier in the morning had abruptly left him, and he'd started to cough again.

'In the North Sea,' said Dell. 'It's just a square on the map, really. But shush now.'

The fifth item on the news was the Bristow story. There was nothing new except a statement from the car depot saying that no one called Bristow had been employed there.

Tony picked up again from the back. 'Isn't that where Daddy works?'

Dell abandoned the pretence he had planned, of listening just as solemnly through the rest of the bulletin. 'Okay,' he murmured to Nancy. 'That's enough.' She switched to music on the Light instead.

'Isn't it?' dinned Tony from force of habit. He didn't really want to know. Nancy looked at him anxiously. The boy had hardly eaten anything and the hollows under his eyes were darkening. 'When you take him to the Gents,' she told Dell, 'keep him wrapped up. He can go in the front then. I think it's warmer. Babba and I'll go in the back.'

'We're nearly there,' said Dell.

They drove on under the high fen sky, the steady fen wind pushing on the slab sides of the car so that Dell had to keep the steering constantly corrected. In the distance, pale against the horizon blur, a slender tower poked up from the flat landscape.

'The Stump,' said Dell. 'Boston Stump.'

'Where?' said Tony dutifully. 'I can't see it.'

'Over there to the left side. Like a tall tower. It's the church at Boston.'

'It's not a stump then. A stump's when you cut something off.'

'That's what they call it, I don't know why. They just do.' But Tony had lolled back in his seat again. Approaching the town Dell started to look out for the landmarks of years before. New housing estates were springing up, rows of little square houses marshalled at the sides of the road, but behind them still the flat, wet fields, and still the remembered lanes winding down to lonely level crossings. Then they were between the Victorian villas of the last half-mile and crossing the railway, passing the swing bridge on one side and the square bulk of the canning factory on the other, through a narrow crowded street and over the Town Bridge into the market place. Dell parked in a side street, opposite a café with a sign in the window that changed oilily from red to green and back to red.

'You and the kids get a warm up and a cup of tea,' he urged Nancy. 'Something to eat, too.'

'What about you?'

'I've got to get on. We've lost too much time already.'

It took Dell a moment to orientate himself. The market place was a great paved Delta, grey and empty in the November afternoon. To his right the long nave and terminal soaring tower of the church made a vast capital 'L'. Beyond it a long row of shops curved round towards the bridge. To his left a cinema proclaiming Electric Pictures, a chain store, more shops and the jutting portico of a hotel led towards the distant apex of the triangle, where the market place finally narrowed to the width of a single street. It was for this street that Dell made.

The wind was colder still. He raised the collar of his donkey jacket. A sheet of newspaper blowing across the square briefly wrapped itself round his leg. He hurried on. The street grew meaner. Tall buildings gave way to Victorian terraces broken by gaps which revealed further terraces tucked behind. Dell crossed an intersection and the street began to change character again: a timber yard, a ship's chandlers store with oilskins and brass fittings in the window, a ship's butchers, a sudden, unexpected little park with tall trees and deep grass, and then he was approaching the docks.

There was no formal entrance. The road divided into three roads which straggled away like branches from an artery. Dell took the right hand branch, passing a tiny hut marked Dock Police, then a low modern labour office and a canteen. He picked his way across railway lines, past a stack of crates, old pallets, the rubbish of a hundred years, heading for the cranes which poked up to the sky from their tall gaunt carriages. A minute later he stood looking at the bleak rectangular basin of the main dock. There were four big ships in. The nearest was loading machinery, a Swedish boat. Dell watched the crane swing a massive crate from a flat-car up, around, and down into the hold. A grimy collier was moored by the blackened machinery of the coal wharf; a white German boat was being hosed down by crew members. Beyond that, in the furthest corner of the basin, was a broad black hull riding low in the water. From the stern fluttered a dingy red flag. Beneath the flag Cyrillic letters spelled a Russian name and a port of registration which Dell, drawing nearer, was able to identify as Tallinn. The wind drew a smear of black smoke from the single funnel. Dell slowed his pace and sauntered past the vessel hands in pockets, looking for signs of life. In case anyone was watching he carried on to the end of the basin, past the lock gates and the green corrugated iron sheds of the harbourmaster and customs service, on to a neck of waste land overlooking the channel which wound away through the fens to the distant sea. The water was low in it now, showing slopes of black mud littered with rusty cans and a half buried tractor tyre. The wind carried a tang of salt here. Dell pulled the donkey jacket closer about him and turned back. As he approached the Soviet ship a fat man in a grey singlet emerged and tipped a bucket of water away. Dell could see the length of the basin wall: no one near, no one looking his way. He quickened his step and called *Hi* to the fat man.

The fat man grunted something in return and began to disappear through an iron door. Dell shouted again, more urgently. The man turned. He had a cheery, thick-lipped face and not much hair. He said *B-rrrrrr* and pointed towards the sea and made a motion of hugging himself and grinned.

Dell said, 'Do you speak English?'

The man nodded vigorously and grinned again.

'Can I see your captain?'

The man went on nodding and grinning, then suddenly said *'Nitvare!*

'*Nitvare?*'

A frown creased the cheery face. The thick lips overlapped in thought. He tried again. 'Tvin-sets. Yompers. Arris-veed.' A hand plunged into a pocket and flourished a wallet.

'Oh, knitwear,' said Dell. 'No, I haven't. But can I see your captain?' He took a pace up the gangplank.

The smile vanished instantaneously. He motioned Dell back vigorously. Dell hesitated, and said, 'Captain eh? *Kapi-tan.*'

The man scratched his head and frowned again and then looked past Dell and the rubbery lips curved in relief. He pointed, Dell spun round. Two figures were approaching from the green hut. The Russian captain had a cap with ear flaps hanging down; the man with him wore a blue mac and a peaked cap and carried an attaché case. Dell thrust his hands in his pockets and moved slowly away, pretending to transfer his attention to a fishing boat tied up across the dock. He heard the men's voices as they drew nearer; they were speaking English, the Russian deep and broken, the other in ordinary tones not loud enough for him to overhear. He felt their eyes on him. Ten yards on he dared a look back. The fat man aboard the ship had disappeared. The captain was shaking hands with the blue mac. Then he clattered aboard his ship and disappeared.

The Swedish ship was still loading. Dell walked round to the collier. She was registered locally but with a Dutch sounding name *Amstel Girl*. Dell looked up and down the quayside and slipped warily aboard. 'Anyone there?' he called. 'Anyone at home?' There was no reply. He forced himself to go aboard.

A chink of light showed under a door in the far corner of the well deck. Dell trod deliberately round to it, trying to avoid the temptation to tiptoe. It was the galley. There was a mug of tea on the table and a newspaper but otherwise the place was tidy, all the equipment hung in place. Dell noticed with vague surprise that the stove was an ordinary, old-fashioned kitchen stove. A bucket of coke stood by it. He picked up the paper. It was the daily stablemate of Hunter's paper, and obviously the one that had sprung the Bristow story. The headline leaped from the page between the inverted commas that signified the news was so far only hearsay, 'MISSING SCIENTIST IS £8 p.w. CAR WORKER' — Report. He dropped the paper as he heard a sudden gush of water, the clang of an iron door. There was a stamping of feet and an angry black face jogged up from below. 'What you doing here?' demanded a voice.

'Nothing,' said Dell. 'I shouted but no one answered.'

'How did you get aboard, then?'

'I just walked.'

'Yeah, well you just walk off again, before I call the dockies. We've had enough stuff lifted from this ship.' He was a coloured seaman in a thick jersey. He grabbed an outsize knife from the rack.

'Listen —' said Dell urgently.

'Look, mister, I don't know who you are but get off.'

Dell retreated to the well deck. The seaman moved to the galley entrance and looked anxiously along the dock. 'Did anyone see you come on?'

'No,' said Dell. 'Look, I only —'

'Get *off*,' hissed the man.

Dell obeyed. From the quayside he said, 'All right, I'm off. Now we can talk?'

'What about?'

'About sailing on this ship. You know, as passenger.'

The seaman looked at him suspiciously. 'I wouldn't know anything about that. You come back when Mr. Selwyn's here maybe.'

'When would that be?'

'I don't know. One hour, maybe. But don't you come walking about like God Almighty. You shout first.'

Dell scuttled away from the docks. Outside the tiny hut a dock policeman was deep in conversation with the man in the peaked cap who'd accompanied the Russian skipper. He looked up as Dell passed and gave him a long stare. The wind was even colder as the daylight faded.

In the market place the shop windows were bright. Dell bought an evening paper and read the headlines as he hurried on. MISSING SCIENTIST IN IRELAND REPORT, and underneath in smaller letters, 'But car plant says: we don't know him.' He beckoned Nancy and the children from the café, and scrambled into the car. He ran the engine while he waited. He opened his mouth to break the bad news.

Nancy said, 'Tony was sick.'

'What?' He swivelled and stared at the little face in the gloom.

'All over their table, and on his coat, too. They were quite nice about it, but —'

'But he's never done that before.'

'I know. He's ill. Can't you see?' She was near to crying. 'You shouldn't have left us all that time.'

Dell let the hand brake off and gazed unseeingly down the street. Automatically he rubbed the windscreen clear.

Nancy whispered, 'Get us out of this. Make it come all right. Make it come all right.'

Dell drove back through the square, over the bridge, through the narrow streets out to the main road again, and turned down the winding country lane through the fens. There, dropped down as if at random among the fields of stinking cabbage and draining ditches, a pattern of low buildings part-enclosed an asphalt playground on which the white lines of a netball pitch stood out boldly in the gloom. Behind the tall windows the big white light globes were going out one by one. In the car the baby who had been dozing in Nancy's arms stirred and clawed herself up as a party of home-going children divided and called shrill goodbyes.

Dell stopped the car and switched off and sat watching the school. After a while a car emerged, then another, then two women walking. Dell peered through the windscreen. Someone was wheeling a bike, fiddling with the front lamp to get it going, a tall woman whose stride, even as she pushed the bike, was unmistakable. Dell opened the car door and let it shut behind him and took a pace forward and said, 'Miss Rayner…'

She said, 'What do you want? Let me get past, please.' She sounded apprehensive.

'It's me, Stella. Don't you remember?'

Dell sat in an armchair and watched the revolving flames endlessly consume the plastic logs. In the warmth from the fire bars below his eyes were heavy and their lids smarted. Upstairs he heard murmured feminine tones, the baby's excited cries, the clip-clop of heels on lino. Stella had recognised him after that first alarm. They'd stood awkwardly for a minute, but without exchanging the usual flat formalities about it being a long time. Stella had looked past Dell's shoulder into the car and looked away and straightened a bundle of books in her bicycle basket and said, 'What are you going to do now?' She seemed about to go. Then she'd suddenly said, 'Well, at least come home and have a warmup,' and Dell had whined along in low gear behind the taillight of her bike as she led the way to one of the little bright boxes in the new estates.

Nancy came downstairs with the baby, dumped her on Dell's lap and vanished into the kitchen. The baby gazed spellbound at the electric logs and said, 'Fah! hot hot Fah!'

'Yeah,' said Dell. 'You're fooled too.' He smelled the fragrance of her little head. She was in pyjamas, ready for bed. Nancy came in again with a bowl of cereal. 'We're not going on tonight, then?' said Dell.

'You know we're not,' she said expressionlessly. 'We've nowhere to go and anyway the kids have had enough. More than enough.'

'How is Tony?'

'He went down all right, but I'm worried. I gave him a double dose of his pills.'

'He hasn't coughed much today, really.'

'In a way I wish he had. At least we know what it is then. She said she'd get her doctor if I wanted...'

'If you like. It would finish things for good, though.'

She didn't reply, but started spooning cereal into the baby. Stella came into the room and collected Dell's tea-cup and then perched on the edge of the settee watching.

She said, 'Susan — that's my friend's little girl I was telling you about — she won't eat Farex or any of those things. Susan has to make old-fashioned porridge for her, that's all she'll touch.' She laughed nervously.

'I know,' said Nancy absently. 'They're funny in their likes and dislikes.'

'Susan doesn't even like Baby Rice.' Her face had become thinner, Dell noticed, and also weathered; the colouring was a young girl's but it had become fixed and dulled, like that of a stored apple. She stared at the baby with eyes that saw nothing else until she abruptly stood up and said, 'I'll just tidy the bathroom.'

There was silence at first when she'd gone. Dell broke it.

'How did you get on with her?'

'She's very kind,' said Nancy coldly. 'She gave me a lot of advice on the proper way to bring up kids.'

'You don't want to take any notice of that. She can't help it. She would have liked some of her own.'

Then Nancy said, after a minute, 'Why did she never marry?'

'I suppose I would have married her if things had turned out differently.'

'You'd have got on well with her, wouldn't you? You'd have had more to talk about together.'

'Oh, for God's sake!' Dell heaved himself out of the armchair and stood over the electric logs. 'Listen, I didn't *want* to marry her. I was getting trapped into it.'

'Ssh,' said Nancy, frowning.

Dell looked down at the logs. 'I keep wanting to kick these things and only just remember not to.' The electric clock on the tiny tiled mantelpiece said 5.30. 'I wonder when Daddy gets in, and what do we say to him?'

'She said he'd be going to the hospital to see Mrs. Rayner and wouldn't be home until after visiting hour.' She offered a cup of warm milk to the baby, who blew bubbles in it. 'Come on, proper drinks, proper drinks.'

Dell said, 'That gives us about two hours before the balloon goes up, then?'

'What do you mean?'

'He'll be dialling 999 before you can say Jack Robinson. Ah, what's the use? We might as well pack it in now. It's been a brave gesture. It didn't come off, that's all.'

Nancy gathered up the baby and came over and stood up to Dell in the stance he knew well, legs apart, head up. She said, 'I flitted with you last night at half an hour's notice — less really, because I thought we were going back home. It was cutting myself off from just about everything I've ever wanted. I did it without being told why and I did it without complaining —'

'Just a minute —'

'Let me finish. I did it because the thing that's more important to me than anything is you and the kids: us. I thought that's what you thought, too. I was prepared for anything that would keep us together, and I still am. I want twelve hours for Tony, that's all I ask, one night in a decent, warm bed; for if he doesn't get it, I don't know what'll happen and that's the truth. Tomorrow morning I'll do whatever you want, I'll go wherever you say. If you want to give up, that's your decision. As far as I'm concerned, nothing's changed. Only that twelve hours; that's all I've asked.' She turned and was gone, the baby looking back over her shoulder and inflating a last milky bubble in the farewell.

Dell remained standing by the fire for a full five minutes. After a while he found his eyes were focused on a framed print of pinky-white magnolias. Abstractedly he counted them, up to eleven. He heard Stella in the kitchen.

She called through, 'Do you want the news on the telly?'

'Oh, yes. If you don't mind.'

'Of course not.' She came in and leaned down to switch on the set at the wall point. Her body had thickened and her legs got thinner.

'Let me,' said Dell belatedly.

'It's done now.' She straightened up with a wince. 'I get these twinges in the back. Age creeping on.' Again the little nervous laugh. 'Mind you, the wind here doesn't help. Goes through you like a knife.'

'I'm sorry about the phone calls last night.'

'From the papers, you mean? It can't be helped. I suppose it's the first reaction you get from that type of journalism — ringing up anyone who once knew a person, even if it's the middle of the night. I was able to say I hadn't heard anything for seven years, so it was quite lucky really.' She gave the mirthless giggle. 'Daddy wasn't very pleased, of course. He hasn't been sleeping well lately, what with Mummy and everything...'

'I heard from the man Hunter that she was in hospital. I was terribly sorry...'

'I'm sure you were. We just have to be brave about her — as brave as she is. She was very fond of you, you know.'

The television set suddenly emitted thunderous music. Stella turned it down. She still had strong, beautiful hands.

She said, 'What have you decided to do, then?'

'Nothing, yet.'

'I can try this friend of mine again if you like.'

'I think it's too late.'

Stella said hesitantly. 'You're very welcome to stay here, of course. The only thing is, I don't know how Daddy will take it. You know what he's like...' The television screen swum with a pattern of light that settled into a picture of a dog licking a boy's face.

'I wouldn't dream of it. We've asked much too much of you already.'

'Tonight you mean? My goodness, I could no more have let those children spend another night out than — than — I don't know what.' A procession of names succeeded the boy and dog.

'You're awfully kind.'

She said, 'The news is next,' and turned the sound up. But first came some commercials. They stared at them in silence. Then the clock hands were reading 5.55 and there was a burst of music and they were looking at Dell's face of seven years before. Stella gasped. A moment later the picture was replaced by the presence of the newsreader. 'The Missing Scientist,' he announced with practised crispness. 'Mr. Godfrey Simmons, Labour M.P. for the Wye boroughs, said today he has firm evidence that John Bristow, the government research worker who disappeared seven years ago has been working in this country for nearly the whole of that time, latterly in a car depot under the name of Dell. But reporters who went to an isolated cottage thirty miles from London where Dell, his wife and two children had been living, found it empty and locked!' And suddenly the screen was smudgily filled with the cottage — their cottage — two or three figures standing disconsolately in the foreground.

Dell heard a sound behind him. Nancy had come in without their noticing. She held the mug that the baby had been using in one hand, a tea-towel in the other. 'Switch it off! ' she said. Her voice was strained. 'They shouldn't show things like that. It's someone's *home* —'

'Sssh,' said Dell. Stella's hand was already reaching for the switch. He signalled to her to leave it. Another voice, not the newsreader's, had taken up the tale.

'…to Reading, where they booked tickets to Dublin by the Fishguard route. But a porter at Reading Station said he was positive no one of this description boarded the train.'

'Meanwhile the Home Office has continued to keep silent' — the newsreader was back. 'Our political correspondent, however, says that whatever the outcome of the mystery it's likely to cause the government considerable embarrassment, with the country's security measures already under severe criticism and a full-scale debate promised for next week.'

'All right,' said Dell. 'That's enough.' In the sudden silence he could hear the hum of the electric clock. 'That boyfriend of yours, Stella — would you mind ringing him after all?'

Dell took the bus into town, preferring to leave the car where they'd put it earlier, in the little brick garage of a neighbour's house. The rendezvous was the hotel in the market place. Dell found his way through to a back bar where a big fire burned in the grate and a girl in a black dress served Scotches and Worthingtons to three Rotarians. He ordered a drink and munched cubes of cheese from a bowl on the bar. The clock ticked up to seven p.m. pub time, which probably meant ten to in reality. Two minutes later the door pushed open and Dell knew for certain it was his man. Unbuttoning his overcoat as he came in, he nodded to the girl and the bar in general while at the same time making it obvious he was looking for someone in particular. He came over to Dell.

'You're the chap Stell phoned me about? Oh, good. I don't know if I can help but I'll try. The name's Harvey, Derek Harvey.'

Dell said, 'What'll you have?'

'A Worthy, thanks.'

Dell sought the attention of the girl in black.

'Stell's a good sort isn't she?' said the newcomer. He had a pleasant, innocuous face. 'We used to go on motor treasure hunts with the Fellowship. You know, you follow clues round the countryside. Then I got keen on golf. You want to go on a ship, she said?'

'That's right.'

'Well, it's not very easy just now. We're agents for about half the ones that use this port regularly — did she tell you? It's my uncle's firm actually, I went in when I came out of the Raff. Anyway, the Garden Line, which is the main one, has more or less clamped down altogether. They had some trouble with the insurance last summer when one of their boats had a shunt off Almaar. We could try writing to the head office, if you like.'

'That wouldn't do, I'm afraid. It has to be tomorrow or not at all.'

'Oh Golly.' He looked at Dell quizzically. 'This is on the level, is it?'

'It's life and death.'

He opened his mouth as if he were going to say something, thought better of it, took a drink instead, and said, 'I see,' then took a deeper drink. 'There's a Russian ship —'

Again he cut himself off.

'I tried a personal approach this afternoon. It didn't work.'

'No, I should think they're pretty sticky. Then there's the Swedish boat, but' — he looked up at the clock — 'she'll be sailing about now. The tide's six-thirty. Is there anywhere special you want to go? I mean — does it have to be…?'

Dell shrugged. 'Anywhere, really.' He nibbled a piece of cheese. 'Holland would be the favourite, I suppose. I could go on somewhere else from there.'

'Well that rather puts us back to the Garden Line. There's only the *Amstel Girl* in at the moment…'

'I tried her, too,' said Dell ruefully.

'She's in for a week, anyway. Most of the crew have gone off. They're fitting a radar set or something.' He frowned with concentration. 'Wait a minute! There's always the old *Posy*. She might be in.'

'What's that?'

'The *Posy*? It's a bit of a joke — the name, I mean. She runs fertiliser across from somewhere up the canal from Zaandam. Usually goes back under ballast.'

'Sounds fine.'

'Well she doesn't *smell* very fine.' He looked pleased with his riposte. He lowered his voice a decibel. 'She's known locally as the shit-boat. Actually, it's not — it's just a sort of powdery stuff called Fish Bone & Blood, smells like any other fertiliser. But she's tiny. Only 250 tons, or something like that, and pretty rough aboard.'

'Who runs her? Who does she belong to?'

'That's where you may be lucky. She's on charter to this fertiliser crowd but she belongs to the skipper himself. So he's a fairly free operator. The thing is, is she in now and where do we find him?' He wrinkled his brow in thought. 'I've never seen him in any of the pubs by the docks — of course he berths at the Riverside Quay which is right at the other end. There's a place just across the square the fishermen use a lot.

We might try that. But what are you going to have — the same again?'

'If it's all the same, I'd like to get going.'

'Of course, of course.'

Harvey had a car outside. They crossed the market place and turned right just before the bridge into a narrow lane. Harvey said, 'What do you think of this town?'

'I like it.'

'It's all right. I thought I'd be bored, you know after travelling around a bit in the Raff. But it's not a bad town. Got a lot of character, lot of life. Maybe it's something to do with being a port, even a little one... This pub, for instance — you can imagine it as a real old smuggler's dive a couple of hundred years ago. I don't know if it ever was ... here we are.'

The pub was tiny. Harvey led the way into a single taproom. There was a bench running round it, a couple of old square tables at one of which two men were playing dominoes. Harvey ordered the drinks and they watched the publican draw them slowly from a row of barrels on a trestle behind him. He was a huge, powerful man, as big and forbidding as Cobb in Dell's pub back home.

Harvey said, 'Does the skipper of the old *Posy* get in here these days?'

The publican squinted at the head on Harvey's pint of bitter. 'Haven't seen him lately. You seen him at all, Joe,' he called.

One of the domino players said, 'That young Dutchie? He usually has the wife and kids aboard. Don't go ashore much. If he does it's Jimmy Streeter's place. I think.'

'That's the North Star up by the Swing Bridge.'

'Thanks.'

They drank up. Dell found he was hurrying, his eye kept straying to an old wall clock with a face tanned brown by centuries of tobacco-smoke. He finished well ahead of Harvey. 'Where is it?' he asked partly to conceal his impatience.

'Through there,' said Harvey pointing to a door. 'But not straight into the river. There's a place!'

Dell pushed through the door. He shivered in the chill dampness of the little courtyard outside. There was a green door with three holes drilled in it high up, and a light above the sign 'GENTS'; some crates and empty bottles, an old pot plant, a dustbin and — beyond an iron railing — the river. Dell took a look. A flight of stone steps led down to the black water six or eight feet below. A moored dinghy bumped rhythmically against the stone work.

'Br-rrr,' he said to Harvey when he went in again. 'I see what you mean about smugglers.'

They drove back down the lane and over the bridge. The North Star was a square, commercial-looking pub past the canning factory. They hadn't seen the Dutch skipper lately, but someone said the *Posy* must have come in on the morning tide. He'd seen her from the bus that afternoon, tied up at the fertiliser company wharf.

'Is there any chance of finding him aboard.'

'Don't see why not.'

In the car again Dell said, 'It's kind of you to take so much trouble for a stranger.',

'Any friend of Stell's a friend of mine. Besides, what's wrong with a pub-crawl at any time?' He drove slowly over a level-crossing and stopped the car, looking round him. 'The trouble is there's nowhere to park, and the road's so damned narrow here. Well, we'll have to chance it for a few minutes.'

They climbed out and on to a muddy grass bank at the side of the road. Harvey said, 'Here's the river again. It comes through the town, round here, then goes in a big curve right round the docks and on to the Wash. That's the Riverside Quay over there — see the warehouse! We get over by the Swing Bridge.'

They plodded along the grass bank to the railway line, past a little octagonal signal box, and followed the rails over the bridge. After a patch of waste land they were in the dock area again, but totally different in character from the busy clutter Dell had found earlier in the day. A few concrete standard lamps threw isolated pools of light. In the darkness between them loomed great stacks of timber, lines of stationary wagons, and not a soul in sight, nothing moving. Railway lines seemed to spread everywhere. Three or four still cranes were silhouetted against the sky.

Harvey, leading the way, caught his toe on something and swore. 'Don't know this end very well,' he muttered. 'I hope the car's all right. You won't mind if I rush off pretty damn quick if we do find him?'

'Of course not. It'd probably be just as well…'

'Quite,' said Harvey.

They were cutting across the wide sweep the river made to rejoin it further downstream. They passed on the left of the warehouse. Dell became aware of a fishy smell.

'Smell it?' said Harvey, as if reading his thoughts.

Then ahead was a line of railway hopper trucks and a tall building that showed dusty white in the light of a single arc lamp raised high on a pole. More light but dimmer, yellower, showed from an open door. In front of it a man was sweeping, sunk inside his overcoat to escape the cold wind.

'Evening,' said Harvey.

The sweeping man peered at them over the parapet of his collar and recognising Harvey returned his greeting.

'Just want a word with the skipper,' said Harvey. 'Is he aboard?'

'Haven't seen him leave.'

Harvey led the way through the shed and out on the other side, on the quay. The high overhead light quivered in the wind so that the shadows it cast trembled too. Only the mast and funnel top of the *Posy* were visible above the quayside. Dell looked over the edge and blinked. He said to Harvey, trying to make a joke of it, 'We went on a river steamer last summer that was bigger than this.'

'Don't say I didn't warn you.'

An ordinary ladder led steeply down to the deck. Harvey swung himself on to it with easy assurance and scrambled down. Dell followed more awkwardly. Harvey was already opening a door. They stepped up into the little wheelhouse, like an old-fashioned railway compartment sliced down the middle. From it a steep companionway led below.

'Anyone at home?' called Harvey.

'Yoh,' said a voice. 'Who wants me?'

'Coming down,' said Harvey. To Dell he muttered, 'Watch your head and your step.'

A sudden warmth enveloped Dell as he descended. The atmosphere was thick with it, along with the smell of tobacco smoke and steam and cooking. Dell followed Harvey through a curtain into a square cabin, roomier than the size of the ship would have seemed to allow. The heat came from a copper stove whose flue pipe reached angularly for a hole in the ceiling across the width of the cabin; a tin washbasin of water steamed on top of it. Dell noticed a litter of clothing, an old teddy bear, a Hollywood magazine that the captain had been reading.

He'd stood up as they crowded in. He was not more than thirty with a lean stormtrooper's face, handsome except for a two-day stubble. He was smoking a flat-bowled pipe. He wore a leather jacket and an old pair of tan twill trousers. He pushed a stool he'd been sitting on towards Harvey. There was also a chair. He spoke in a slightly nasal accent 'I'm sorry you catch me like a gangster. I was just going to shave.' He indicated the bowl of water.

'Carry on,' said Harvey. 'We won't keep you a minute. This is a friend of mine, er …'

'Robertson,' said Dell. 'John Robertson.'

The captain inclined his head. 'Please sit down.' He reached over to a wall cupboard with a sliding door and pulled out a bottle and little glasses. Dell couldn't help noticing they hadn't been washed out very well. The captain filled each with a pink liquor.

'Cheers,' said Harvey.

It was some sort of cherry brandy, tasting of almonds. Dell didn't much care for it. The captain re-filled the glasses.

Harvey said, 'Good trip across?'

'Yoh, not bad. The wind was strong, so we miss the tide last night, come in this morning instead. But not bad.'

'Is the missus with you this time? The nippers.'

'No, she thought it was getting too rough. Maybe next time if the wind drops.'

Harvey drained his glass and covered it with his hand, in mute refusal of more. 'Mr. Robertson's wondering if there's any chance of a trip back with you…'

The captain drew on his pipe.

Dell said, 'It would depend when you were going, rather.'

'Yoh, if we get the unloading finished tomorrow by twelve I'll go on the evening tide. But the men don't work after twelve on Saturday, you know.' He eyed Dell more closely. 'If that's any good to you I think it would be okay.'

'It could hardly be better.'

'Good,' said Harvey briskly. 'Now if you don't mind I'll leave you to settle details among yourselves. I've got a car along at the main road where a bus is going to bash into it any minute.' To the captain he said, 'Thanks a lot, old man.' To Dell he whispered, 'Slip a quid to the cook when you get there. No need to offer anything to the skipper himself.'

'I can't begin to thank you —'

'Don't mention it. Give my regards to Stella, have a nice trip, and' — he winked — 'I don't know anything about it, eh?' He disappeared up the companionway.

The skipper said, 'You should bring a blanket if you can. It's cold at night and we haven't so many on the ship.'

'Sure,' said Dell. He looked the other man in the eye, wondering how to spring the next bit.

'Smoke?' The skipper pushed a packet of American-type cigarettes towards him.

'No thanks.' He could delay no longer. 'I might as well tell you. I have reasons for wanting to get away. But I give you my word the police aren't after me or anything like that…'

The skipper knocked out his pipe on the stove and reached for a cigarette with the other hand. 'I can do without any trouble at the moment. I bought this ship on a loan, you know? I'm paying back at four hundred gulden a month. Miss a couple of trips and I'd be…' He gestured expressively.

Dell said, 'I'll tell you the worst. No hedging. I haven't got a passport. I want to take a wife and two children with me. I'm not on the run from the police. I am on the run from the Press — you know, the newspapers. I did something a long time ago, now they're discovering me all over again.'

The skipper lit his cigarette with a stormproof lighter that yielded a flame like a blow lamp's. 'The yournalists, eh? Yoh, I

117

know them.' He snuffed the flame with the lighter cap. 'But it gets more difficult with everything you say. No passport, wife and children!'

'One's only a baby.'

'We've got two. The girl is two and a half, the boy is only born since March.' But the remembrance of them added to his unease. 'I think I can't do it, you know. It's trouble at the other end as well as here.'

Dell said, 'I don't expect you to take risks for a stranger. I'd be willing to — er — contribute something.'

'Yoh? How much?'

Dell hesitated. 'Forty pounds?'

The skipper shook his head.

'Well what then?'

He shrugged. 'A hundred, maybe. But I still don't like it. This is only a little port but they have Customs and everything. Come aboard and seal the duty-free locker the moment we tie up, all that. Once they searched the whole ship.'

Dell said, 'I could make it a hundred, at a pinch.'

'Yoh.' He thought for a moment. 'I guess the wife and children wouldn't be too hard. We usually have someone's family aboard, mine or the engineer's. They're used to hearing a baby crying below.' He poured two glassfuls of the pink stuff, corked the bottle and put it away. 'If I did take you and the police or anyone like that came, you wouldn't say anything about the money? I could say I was just doing it for Mr. Harvey and didn't know anything?'

'Of course,' said Dell confidently.

The skipper reached a decision. 'I tell you, I must ask the engineer what he thinks. He's ashore now. Can you meet us tomorrow when we knew the unloading's finished?'

'All right. What time?'

'About one o'clock, eh? You know the North Star inn? — no, wait a minute, we have to first see the agents. The hotel in the market place? Okay. We drink to that.'

They drained the little glasses and the skipper showed Dell out a different way, through a little galley and round a catwalk between the wheelhouse and the cargo hatches. They shook hands. The skipper sniffed the wind. He said, 'If it gets up too much, no one will be sailing at all.'

'Oh God.' Dell's face fell.

'But I think maybe it will be all right.'

Stella said, 'Derek was able to help, then? It was Derek?' It was obviously very important to know that, to be able to share in the credit.

'Yes, yes,' said Dell truthfully. 'It was all thanks to him. Of course, it's not definite yet —'

'He is nice, isn't he? I'm so pleased.' She withdrew a casserole dish from the oven, holding it in a cloth which had compartments for the hands at each end; her face was slightly flushed and she did look pleased, also pretty. She added, 'Daddy'll be pleased, too. Are you ready for this now?'

'Thank you, yes. Can I have it out here?'

'Oh no, come through. Daddy should hear the good news, too.'

'If you don't mind. I'd rather he didn't … not just yet…'

'Of course.' Stella's voice went momentarily cold. 'I wouldn't dream of telling him anything confidential.' The sound of the television in the living room came funnelling in as she opened the serving hatch and pushed the casserole through and shut the hatch again. 'Come and eat now.'

Nancy, in a borrowed apron, tugged Dell's sleeve as he was about to follow. 'I knew you'd do it.' She whispered, 'I knew you'd fix something.'

'Don't count on it too much, that's all.'

Rayner pushed himself out of his armchair as they entered and turned off the television with a flourish, as if it were something he'd been brought up to do by strict parents, like opening a door for a lady. He was a grey little man who looked lop-sided. He had lost all his teeth on one side of his mouth and had never replaced them with artificial ones. He held his head askew to talk and kept his mouth closed on the empty side, both devices to conceal the hole in his head. He extended a hand that always seemed dry and dusty and said, 'It's been a long time, John.'

'I know.'

'You should have brought your good wife to come and see us earlier. The children, too. Mrs. Rayner would have liked to see them. She was always fond of children.'

'Oh, *Daddy*!' said Stella. 'Don't put her into the past tense yet.'

Rayner allowed an expression of pain to cross his face. 'There's no need to be so sharp, Stella.'

'How *was* Mrs. Rayner?' asked Dell hastily.

'As well as may be expected. She's a very brave woman, you know.'

'John must eat his supper before it gets cold,' said Stella.

The tablecloth had been folded back to cover just one end of the table in the dining end. A single place was set. Dell sat down and began to eat. In the warmth his eyes were suddenly heavy. By the fireside Stella began a long monologue about something that happened at school. Nancy listened with seeming attentiveness but twice she stifled a yawn, Rayner distractingly divided his attention between what was going on in the room and what was still going on, to a ghostly, muted sound accompaniment, on the television screen. Dell craned his head to make sure it wasn't another news bulletin.

Stella, noticing, said, 'Oh, Daddy, do have the thing on properly or not at all. I'm sure John and his wife won't mind

Rayner mumbled something from behind sheltering lips.

'Don't worry about us,' said Dell coolly. 'In any case, I should think Nancy would want to go up soon. We didn't have much sleep last night, one way and another…'

'Oh, I'm *sorry*.' Stella jumped up. 'I should have guessed. There's a bottle in your bed, Nancy, but I'll get you a fresh one to take up. John, you know you'll be on the settee — Tony's in the little box room — I'm sorry we don't have a proper spare room but we don't get… Her voice became indistinct as she reached the kitchen.

Rayner said, 'Well, if you're sure you don't mind,' and reached for the volume control, the sound of urgent American voices swelled up.

After a moment, Nancy rose to go. 'I'll say good night then Mr. Rayner.'

Rayner struggled to his feet. 'If you turn the thing down again,' Dell muttered, 'I'll scream.' Rayner turned it down. He said vaguely, 'Let us know if there's anything you need, won't you.'

Nancy gave Dell a peck. 'Good night, love.'

Dell squeezed her arm. 'See you in the morning.'

She whispered, 'This is the first time we've not been together.'

'I know.'

When she'd gone, Rayner didn't at first turn up the sound again. Hovering over the set, he said into the electric fire as much as to Dell, 'Stella never shows her feelings very strongly but I know she was — well, fond of you. Other things being equal — I mean, with your job, and so on, would you have married?'

'I suppose so.'

'That's as I thought. I only hope she understands so herself. It wouldn't be nice for her to think that she was spurned merely in favour of a woman who simply happened to be more — more physical.'

Dell goggled.

'Especially,' said Rayner, 'one from a rather different class.'

Dell struggled to frame a coherent reply. 'I've never heard anything so —'

Rayner quietly cut him off. 'Just a minute, just a minute, I haven't finished. I've deliberately not gone into what else happened seven years ago, despite the fact that it is once more the subject of speculation. Stella may have told you how we were harassed the other night. It seems nothing very creditable but Stella has always remained completely loyal to you. And as long as you're a guest in this house I shan't pry. I merely wanted you to realise what you may have done to her, turning up after all these years, she still not married and now unlikely to be, you with a wife and children. I must admit that at the moment she seems to be enjoying your visit. She has not been so lively for some time. It is when you are gone again that worries me.'

Dell's fury subsided. He said, 'I'm sorry, I had no idea ... after so long...'

But Rayner was already turning up the sound and it was as if he at the same time turned down Dell. He retreated to his chair again and immersed himself in the intelligence from the screen.

It was ten-thirty on the electric clock. The settee had been made up with a pillow, sheets, a thick tartan rug. Dell pulled on his pyjamas and listened anxiously to the wind that fretted round the eaves and gently swayed the long curtains across the French windows at the back of the room. There was a tap on the door.

'Yes?'

'It's only me.' Stella came in. She was in a long quilted dressing-gown. 'I usually have a cup of Horlicks or something like that last thing. I wondered if you'd like one…'

'I'm pretty sleepy already, thanks.'

'Of course you must be. I'll say good night, then.'

'No, stay. I didn't mean it as a hint. Have yours here. I'll only listen to that damned wind otherwise, or wonder about Tony, or look at the clock and calculate that in twenty-one hours, maybe, we'll…' He let the sentence peter out.

'It's not really a clock, Daddy always says; just a slave dial from the electric company.' She gave her little nervous laugh, before going on. 'Do you remember how we used to go for walks round the docks and pretend we were trying to escape from an occupied country, and how easy it would be to jump on a ship…?'

'It's what gave me the idea of coming here.'

'I thought it must have been. I've often wondered why you didn't try it at the time … instead of that idea about Spain…'

Dell reached out and took her hand. 'Look, if I've upset you, turning up again out of the blue … I never thought…'

'Don't be silly. It's been lovely to see you all. I think Nancy's a sweet person.' She blinked, and when she continued her voice held a high, tight casualness that wasn't casual at all. 'That time before … I've often wondered why you didn't come back? After the hue and cry had died down, I mean…'

Dell said, 'I don't know. I've been trying to think. I went in a panic, without planning anything. But I suppose I thought it would blow over sooner or later.' He paused. 'And then…'

'Then what?' She had a terrible urgency to know.

'I don't know.' He could smell the sandalwood soap she still used, feminine yet antiseptic. 'It just seemed harder and harder to come back.'

She turned away and stared into the fire. In slippers she'd always seemed smaller, somehow more appealing. She said, 'Because of the spy thing or because of me?'

But Dell was listening to something else. '*Sssh!*' He gripped her hand.

Outside there was the sound of a car. It stopped. A door slammed. Stella looked up at Dell in alarm. There was the tread of footsteps on the path and a moment later, the three chimes of the doorbell.

'Answer it,' Dell whispered. He followed her into the hall and slipped into the kitchen, closing the door behind him. He heard Stella call upstairs. 'It's all right, Daddy, I'm going,' then the front door being opened, a loud familiar voice, Stella's reply, the familiar voice suddenly hushed.

After a further exchange on the doorstep Stella led the way into the living room. Dell cautiously opened the serving hatch a crack and listened. Hunter was saying, 'I'm really very sorry to disturb you again, Miss Rayner, but my paper would like a quote from you now that we know Bristow was living in this country all the time,' and she was objecting, 'We've already been rung up in the middle of the night by your office, it's too bad…'

Dell closed the hatch. The tension which had seized him began to ease. He became aware of his heart thumping away.

He tiptoed to the back door and inched the bolt back to make an emergency exit and composed himself to wait patiently.

Within three minutes he had stiffened for action again. This time it was a sound he heard almost before it came. His ear was long attuned to the pattern, the silent exhalation that seemed to come from only a few feet away, the cry, the coughing, the cry again. He darted through the door and up the stairs in his stockinged feet. Tony had his arms up, bent and flailing jerkily as if to ward off something. Dell whispered soothingly, 'It's all right, it's all right,' and got his hands under the thin shoulders to turn him more on his side, and stroked the hot little head.

Tony said, 'A drink.' It was hard to tell if he was awake or not.

'All right. In a minute.'

'A drink!'

'Sssh.' Dell straightened up, listened. He could still hear the mumble of voices below. He set off down the stairs. As he reached the foot, the living room door was jerked open and Hunter said with mild surprise. 'A funny thing — I had an idea you might have come this way.'

Stella, behind him, started to explain, 'He's not —'

Dell pushed past, bumping Hunter with his shoulder, snapping, 'Forget it. I've other things to worry about.'

They followed him into the kitchen. Stella asked, 'What was the trouble?'

'The usual. Temperature. Bad dream. Couldn't get his breath. One of those things or all three. I'll give him a drink and an aspirin.'

'There's some orange juice in the fridge Nancy was giving them.'

'Thanks. Keep an eye on our friend here.'

Hunter said, 'That won't be necessary, as Miss Rayner's been trying to tell you.'

Dell ignored him, but padding up the stairs again he heard Hunter treading carefully in pursuit. In the little cramped room he propped up Tony in the crook of his arm and held the cup to his lips. He was aware that Hunter was looking on.

Tony looked up and said in a small clear voice, 'Did you come in your car?'

Hunter said, 'Yes, I did, Tony. It's outside.'

'We have a red car with windows.'

There was a creak from the door across the landing and Nancy appeared. She was in her best white nylon nightie and her body showed through pink and shadowy. She blinked, only half awake and said, 'What is it?'

'It's all right. Nothing. Go back to bed.' Dell pushed her into her room and then closed Tony's door. 'Go sleepy now, Tone.'

Hunter said, as they went downstairs, 'How is he?' He sounded troubled and insecure.

'He'll live,' said Dell sourly. 'No thanks to you. If anything should happen to these kids by God I'll come back from — from Siberia if necessary, and I'll hound you the way you've hounded us.'

Hunter spun round. His face was dark, his voice thick. 'Listen, can't you see beyond the end of your idiot nose? I'm as fed up with it as you are. You can look after yourself but do you think I want to see that girl and those children hunted like bloody animals? Because that's what it's going to be like tomorrow!'

'What do you mean?' Dell stared at Hunter. The question rang in the stillness of the house.

'We'd better go into the room,' said Hunter.

Stella was already there. She looked at them apprehensively. Dell said, 'Has your Pa got such a thing as a drink in the house? We need one badly.'

'I'll have a look.' She kneeled and rummaged in the sideboard.

Dell said to Hunter, 'I'm sorry for the outburst.'

'That's all right.' Hunter flopped down on the settee. He looked tired. There was a gap in the welt of his shoe where the stitching had come undone. His shirt-cuffs were frayed. There was blue stubble on his chin. His face seemed to sag a bit, his body to slump downwards into his suit. He said, 'As I was trying to explain earlier, they took me off your story and put the toughies on to it, once it got big. I was sent up here simply to get a few fresh reactions from Miss Rayner —'

'You can call me Stella.' She'd found a bottle of port and was filling two little mock-Jacobean tumblers.

'I came along tonight because I guessed the other papers might get around to it tomorrow and I thought I might as well be first. Thanks.' He took the glass Stella handed to him and swallowed half the contents in one gulp. 'I think the possibility exists that they'll still do that. You may as well be warned. It depends a lot on how the main pursuit goes. Your Irish ruse worked quite well, but it was more or less written off by about midday. Then you had some bad luck. The man who sold you a little red station wagon —'

'Doggett?'

'Yeah, Doggett. He read something or heard something and put two and two together. He didn't know who to tell, but he's a *Sketch* reader apparently, so he told them. The *Sketch* hits the Street earlier than most, so it was common knowledge by seven, when I was about to take off. They'd also rung up all the police they could think of, and you'd been pretty definitely traced as far as Cambridge.' He held out his glass and Stella refilled it.

'To digress,' continued Hunter. 'I owe you some sort of explanation for the bloody thing getting out in the first place. Apparently the office fed it to the tame M.P. so that he could table a discreet question and whip up a bit of preliminary curiosity. It helps when you've got this kind of hark-back story. Something went wrong. Probably he got stoned in the Press bar. Anyway it leaked to the Daily and you know the rest.' He lit a cigarette. 'One thing to your good is that so far we've hung on to our pictures which means no one else really knows what you look like now. Incidentally Joe Milton isn't very pleased with you

'The photographer?'

'The very one. He says you smashed some gear that was worth fifty quid. He came shouting into the feature writer's room as if I'd been personally responsible. I can tell you, your stock went up about six points…'

Dell said, 'But what will happen next?'

Hunter drew deeply on his cigarette. His long upper-lip seemed to be squeezing the smoke from it. 'Well, to be frank, you couldn't have chosen a more conspicuous little car. Red with windows, said Tony. That's about it. Every paper will have a picture of some sort tomorrow, and there's always one or two sharp-eyed buggers who know to reverse the charges to Fleet Street and leave their names and addresses in the hopes of a cheque or a plug. You know, *Express* reader Smith dials FLE 8000 and helps trap a spy…'

Dell shrugged. 'I didn't have much chance of shopping around. It happened to come at just the right moment.'

'Where is it now?'

'Next door garage,' said Stella.

'Reliable people?'

'Well, they seem quite pleasant —'

'Mmm. What had you planned to do with it?'

'I was going to sell it,' said Dell.

'*What?* Are you crazy?'

'I need the money.'

Hunter deliberated. He started to pull the black overcoat round him and button it up. He said, 'I'm not going to ask you your plans, then there won't be any misunderstandings. But I'm staying at the hotel — what's it called? — the one in the market place. Give me a ring if you need my help and feel you can trust me; if you can't … well, don't.'

The imitation flames licked endlessly at the plastic logs. Stella sipped her milk drink. Dell stared absently at her feet in fluffy mules beneath the long quilted dressing-gown. They were big feet, at least size eight. He forced his attention back to the yellow AA book on his lap and the scrap of paper on which he had been making a list:

TONY?
WIND?
CAR?
£ s.d.

'What have you decided?'

'Nothing yet. There are so many imponderables.' He took the pencil and added another: ENGINEER? He thought for a minute and drew a stroke through TONY? then impatiently crumpled the paper and threw it at the make-believe fire.

CHAPTER 5: SATURDAY

Dell propped the letter against the electric clock and picked up the old hold-all and looked around the room to make sure he'd forgotten nothing. It was still dark as he let himself out of the sleeping house. He shivered in the raw cold. The door to the neighbour's garage swung up with a squeak from the mechanism and tugging at the rear bumper he rolled the little car down the short driveway and into the road. Leaning through the driver's window to get at the wheel he pushed it as far as the corner before climbing in and starting the engine. On full choke it caught at second attempt, revving up with its characteristic whine. He let in the clutch carefully for the sake of the elastic bands and drove off.

The town was deserted save for some lorry traffic and the inexplicable cyclist who pedals through every town in the small hours. Dell took the road out to the north. As the light grew strong enough to see the landscape he was leaving the fens and running into the gentle undulations of the Wolds. He passed hamlets of a few cottages, occasional trim little country houses with plain elevations and yellow front doors, but not another vehicle, nor even another human being. Pasturelands and newly-ploughed fields tilted away on either side.

At a village called Ludborough he forked off the main road on to a B-road, still heading north, even lonelier than the last. At Ulceby he stopped and frowned over his map. The roads were badly signed and rough from frost damage. The off-side rear suspension had ceased to drum and now only made an ugly grating noise. The whole car had developed a list. Twice Dell cursed as he thought he was on the wrong road. Once he had to brake and reverse to take a turning he'd missed. But at last he came to a sign that said New Holland and presently he was driving between bleak railway-brick villas. At the end of a deserted main street a further sign directed him to a road that led bumpily through a goods siding and, without surprise, to the end of the world.

The estuary stretched away like a sea, white with choppy waves. The far side, the skyline of the city was a grey blur, only the tallest dockyard cranes standing out distinctly. Dell stopped the car and surveyed the desolate scene. A traffic light at green immediately ahead invited him on to the pier which clanked out on piles a quarter-mile into the river, and Dell started to pull away towards it, but then braked again and reversed to the side of the approach. He switched off the engine and climbed out. The wind caught him at once. It blew steadily, chillingly, hostilely.

There was a little railway station to his right, labelled New Holland Town. The line led on along the pier, flanked on one side by the single vehicle carriage way, on the other by a footway. Dell found a booking office and inquired when the first ferry was to Hull.

'Seven-twenty,' said the clerk.

Dell looked at the clock. It was just before seven. 'How much to take a car over?'

'Book at the other end.'

'But how much would that be?'

'Depends on the size. What car you got?'

Dell pointed. 'That little red wagon over there. Can you see? It's twelve or thirteen feet.'

He craned his head. 'About a quid.'

'*Phew*!' Dell made a face.

'If you're coming back this way,' said the man, more amiably, 'you can leave it in the car park instead. It'll cost you a bob.'

'Thanks. I'll do that.'

He retrieved the car, parked it behind the station, extracted the hold-all and without looking back set off along the pier. As he left the shoreline the wind increased in steadiness and force. It pushed him towards the railway line, it blew into his ear so coldly that he had to clap his hand over in protection, it moaned through the under structure, it sent the spray whirling from the waves.

At the end was another little station; as Dell reached it a diesel car rumbled hollowly along the pier and drew up. Dell bought a single ticket to Hull and followed the passengers who, hunching their shoulders against the blast, tramped morosely down the long sloping ramp to the waiting ferry boat. He wedged himself in a sheltered spot on the deck and stared at the distant towers and cranes as the bell rang, gangplanks rattled and the paddlewheels slowly began to turn.

The shop was a scruffy one but behind the dirty glass the window was piled high with silver, a great mound of teapots, inkstands, cutlery, vases, hot water jugs, coins, rose bowls, some still polished, some tarnished and blackened and flattened. A notice said, 'We pay for your unwanted gold and silver,' and another one, 'Sovereigns — today's price: 69/6d.'

Dell pushed in with a jangle from the bell and emptied the cotton bag on the counter. An old grey man in a shapeless cardigan scooped them up without looking at Dell, examined one closely, and retreated into an inner room. There was the sound of a safe being opened. Presently he padded back and swivelled a ledger across the counter, pointing with a blue finger where Dell was to sign and give his name and address. Dell put 'Robert Hunter' and an invented street in London.

Next, a public lavatory: Dell had a quick shave and ran a comb through his hair. He invested a penny in a toilet cubicle, hung the old donkey jacket behind the door and let it swing to. In the street again he walked briskly to keep warm until he found a surplus store with a rack of coats and waterproofs swinging in the wind under the awning. He picked the warmest he could find that seemed to fit, pretending to be a foreigner, shaking his head at the shopkeeper and letting the man count out the money from the fistful he offered.

At the Paragon Station he had time for a cup of coffee and a roll before catching the London train. The booking office was fairly busy. He judged it safe to book only as far as Grantham.

He was on the last lap. The diesel worked its way through the flat fenland, stopping at each tiny station; sometimes no one got off or on; the silence was broken only by the rumble of the motors, the buzz of the guard's signal, the motorman's answering buzz. Level crossing succeeded lonely level crossing, a single delivery van waiting at the gates, a plume of smoke streaming from the chimney of the keeper's house. But the wind seemed to be dropping and sunlight streamed through the railcar windows on to Dell, persuading his head to loll and his eyes to close…

He forced himself into wakefulness. He was sitting in the very front of the front car, with only the motorman in his glass box of a cabin between him and the rails which stretched ahead unwaveringly to the horizon. He regarded the back of the motorman's head. There was a place, perhaps a scar, half an inch long and shaped like a fish, where no hair grew and the skin was chalk white; there was a yellow pencil stub behind his ear; at halts he sipped tea from the plastic cap of the battered thermos flask that stood on the flat dashboard; from the pocket of his green overall jacket projected a folded *Daily Mirror*, showing just a corner of the retouched picture, just a section of the headline which demanded, HAVE YOU SEEN THIS CAR?

They were stopping at the smallest halt of all. There was nothing there but a narrow lane, three leafless trees, a stone house; but washing fluttered from the line and outside the house two children were playing in the sunshine with a yellow puppy whose little shrill barks reached the train a moment after his little head had been thrown back to utter them. Then the buzzer buzzed. They moved on through the fields of potatoes and fields of beet and intersecting dykes towards the slender, beckoning tracery of the Stump.

There was a phone box outside the station. Dell got an engaged signal from the Rayner number, walked up and down biting his nails, tried again. Stella answered with a guarded, 'Yes.'

'It's me.'

Stella hesitated. Then her voice sounded firm and decisive. 'I'm sorry I can't talk to you now. I've got a houseful of reporters already. You'll have to call me back.'

Dell said, 'What about —?'

'I'm not talking on the phone.' Faintly yet clearly Dell heard a voice in the background, 'If it's the *Pic* tell them to try getting up in the morning.'

Dell said urgently, 'Where are they?'

Stella paused again. For a moment Dell thought she'd gone, then he heard another background laugh. She spoke quickly. 'Oh, Mr. Hunter? Just a minute.' There was another pause and then Hunter's voice.

'Hunter here.'

'What's happened?' hissed Dell.

'Oh, hello, old boy. You're a bit late on the scene. Where did you get to?'

'Hull. I left the car at New Holland and caught the ferry —'

'Did you? That would have been a good story, a very good story indeed. Unfortunately it's rather been superseded, old boy. Everyone's flocking to Boston. You see, old man Rayner spilled the beans. The story's still running. Anything could happen. Don't despair. Now listen, your office phoned. The people you want to see will be where you left them yesterday afternoon — is that clear?'

'I think so,' in a whisper.

'What? Okay. And you know where I'll be, old boy.' He rang off.

The station was in a side street away from the centre of the town. Dell had to pause a moment outside and work out his bearings. He half approached a taxi but as the driver started to put down his paper, changed his mind and hurried away on foot. The sun still shone but in the open its warmth was illusory. Dell found his way to the market place. It was market day and he had to side-step impatiently through the stalls and crowds of shoppers. The café with its melting green and red sign was crowded. Dell pushed open the door, breathing but hardly noticing the warm, fish and chippy air. There was no Nancy, no kids. He became aware of the woman behind the cash desk eyeing him with uncertain recognition.

'Was that your wife and little ones that was here?'

'Yes, that's right.'

'They said they'd be in the shops. In the Woolworths or the Marks. They waited here ever such a long time, but you see we wanted the tables for lunches.'

135

'Yah, okay,' said Dell. 'Thanks very much.'

'I mean, it being Market Day and everything —' her reproachful tones followed him out in the street again. 'And I say! There's your luggage here cluttering up behind the counter.'

'Oh, sorry!' Dell went back and waited while someone paid, two luncheon vouchers and a few pennies, that was all. 'I mean we don't mind obliging but Saturdays we *are* crowded, you know.' She stopped and heaved under the counter. Dell took the bulging fibre suitcase, the basket tied with string with the pink pot peeping from the top, Tony's little attaché case. 'I think that's all,' said the woman, puffing. Dell got the basket under his arm and the other pieces as best he could, and retrieved his own hold-all and pushed his way red-faced into the street. The church clock was striking the hour. Dell listened with fresh panic. It was one o'clock.

He pushed his way into the muggy confectionery smell of Woolworths, struggling with the swing doors. They were not there. In the cooler, more spacious Marks & Spencer they were standing under a sign advertising boy's pullovers & socks. Nancy had the baby in her left arm; Tony, muffled in his scarf, hung listlessly on her other hand. She looked weighed-down and exhausted.

'Where've you been?' she said to Dell. 'We waited and waited.'

'Didn't you have any dinner, then? You should have had some dinner.'

'I didn't know whether to or not. You didn't say. We just had drinks and biscuits.'

'And all this bloody luggage. Couldn't you have stowed it somewhere?'

She looked up at him with gathering anger. 'What was I supposed to do with it? You didn't say. You didn't say anything about what we were to do.' Catching the tone of her voice the baby started to cry. Dell felt Tony's hand on his coat and remembered his good resolutions. 'I'm sorry.' There was a press around him, and voices complaining. With the luggage they were blocking half the aisle. He picked up the cases. Tony said, 'Which are my fireworks in?'

'Oh, I forget. They're in one of them,' he lied, and to Nancy, 'How is he?'

'So, so,' she added. 'You got a new coat.'

'I know. Come on.'

'What's the hurry?'

'I've got to meet someone.'

Dell barged his way into the street. Tony took the attaché case, holding it grimly with both hands. Nancy took the basket. Dell said, 'The first thing is to dump this luggage.' They struggled across the market place to the bus stops on the other side. Lunchtime had thinned the crowd slightly. There was no proper bus station, only an enquiries office, but they persuaded the clerk to stow the bags behind the counter.

'Now,' said Dell. 'I've got to meet someone. You go on into the church with the kids. I'll join you there as soon as I can.'

'Don't leave us again,' she implored.

'I can't help it.'

'What about the baby? I've got to change her. The pad must be sopping. She'll catch cold in this weather if I don't change her.'

Dell looked around wildly. 'Wasn't there a Ladies in the café? I don't see anything round here.'

'I didn't like to ask. Besides, there's Tony —'

'Well, you'll have to manage somehow. I'm late already. I'll be as quick as I can.' But he watched them for a moment going on their way, Nancy in the old green coat she should have thrown away years before, Tony trailing half a pace behind with his uncertain gait and his mac belt twisted and one sock sinking down his thin leg, the baby's face hooded in the red flying suit looking back over Nancy's shoulder at nothing in particular, two dots for eyes and a tiny mouth — the picture stayed frozen and fixed as he hurried towards the hotel, dimly aware of the sound of bells filling the air.

In the foyer the first thing he saw — and heard — was a tweed-suited man wedged inside the tiny phone kiosk with one foot holding the door open to let his cigarette smoke escape. He was dictating into the phone loudly and painstakingly, as if to someone hard of hearing. 'Paragraph. All along this cheerless marshy coast from Immingham and Grimsby in the north to Kings Lynn and Wells across the Wash, cap double-u ay, ess for sugar, aitch — okay, okay, I was only making sure — watch is being kept…'

Dell shrank back in dismay. But otherwise the place didn't seem particularly busy. He scurried through to the back bar and peered obliquely through the door. There were only three or four customers, none very animated. The skipper of the *Posy* was leaning against the far end of the bar. With him was a round, fat man sucking a wet cigar that had gone out. He was coatless, with his jacket collar turned up and a woolly hat crammed on his head. He was busy turning out the contents of a trouser pocket on to the bar. His face was screwed up into red concentric circles of concentration.

Dell panted, 'I'm sorry if I'm late.'

The skipper said, 'We only just got here. We had a drink with the agents at the other place.' He struck a match and sucked at his pipe.

'Maurits,' said the fat man, shooting out his hand. He had finished his pocket emptying.

'He's the engineer,' explained the captain. 'It's his cabin you'd have.'

Maurits nodded his head vigorously and said something in Dutch.

'It's all right, then?' said Dell.

The skipper finished lighting his pipe and tossed the box of matches to Maurits. He said slowly. 'Well, I guess it's okay. As long as they don't start searching all the ships or anything special like that. The agents said nothing about there being a lookout for anyone. Only Maurits here he feels he'd be in trouble if anything went wrong. I mean for saying the woman and children were his, you understand?'

Dell fingered the wad of notes in his pocket. He said, 'It depends on how much he'd want…'

'Yoh. I ask him.' He spoke rapidly in Dutch. Maurits pushed back the woollen hat and scratched his head. He was bald except for a fringe of black hair. He picked up his glass and drained it off.

Dell said, 'What was it?'

The skipper said, 'Rum. We drink rum against the cold.' Dell ordered three from the same girl in black who'd been behind the bar the previous evening. Maurits pulled his hat forward again, shrugged elaborately and muttered one word.

'Twenty?' said the skipper. 'Twenty pound?'

Dell hesitated, not to seem too relieved. 'Okay.'

'Good.' Maurits' face cracked into a wide smile. He raised his glass, with a flourish so that the rum splashed in the glass and some of it went on to his dirt-engrained hands. 'Hooray,' he said. They drank. The rum was treacly and warming. Maurits hiccupped and launched into English. 'I look after your wife … nice, eh?' He slapped the skipper on the shoulder and laughed.

'Yeah,' said Dell sourly. He asked the skipper. 'The wind is dropping, isn't it?'

'Yoh, I think it will be okay. But colder. She's coming from the east now.'

Maurits licked the traces of rum off his hand and hailed the girl in black. The captain grabbed his arm and pulled it down and shook his head to countermand the order. 'Don't forget we sail tonight,' he said in English. To Dell he added, 'It's okay for the wife and children to come aboard this afternoon. I wish it you don't come yourself until maybe six o'clock — just in case.'

The captain shrugged. 'It's more safe. You know just supposing they did search the ship or something.' He finished his drink. 'The wife and children are near?'

'They're waiting in the church...' He jerked a thumb in the direction.

'Good. I think it's best they go with Maurits. But when you come yourself come by the Swing Bridge, eh?'

'All right.' Dell made a quick survey of the other customers, checking to see if they seemed to be listening. The girl in black moved down their end. He asked her. 'Busy, eh?'

'Yes, quite.' She was breaking out ice-cubes from a freezer tray into an insulated bowl.

'Did you get all the newspaper fellows in?'

'There were a few. They went haring off somewhere, except for one who's been on the phone out there for the past half hour. They'll be back.'

'What's that?' said the skipper curiously.

'Nothing except that I don't want to hang around here. It wasn't a very bright place for me to come to.'

'Okay, we go now.' The skipper knocked out his pipe and helped himself to a little cigar from the tin Maurits had put on the bar with his other belongings.

Dell said, 'How about this?' He showed him covertly the bundle of a hundred one-pound notes he'd made up with a rubber band. The skipper nodded and he slid it across. Dell said, 'I'll square up with Maurits later.'

'Sure.' He muttered a word or two of Dutch, hunched himself into his coat and was gone … Maurits had started to collect his odds and ends together. Now he winked conspiratorially and made a gesture of raising a glass to his lips.

'No, come on.'

Maurits grinned and held up one grimy finger. 'Chust one more, eh?' he said thickly.

The girl in black set up two little glasses and looked enquiringly at Dell. 'Oh, all right,' he said with bad grace. 'But *schnell*, eh?'

Outside the man in the phone box was finishing his call at last. Dell heard him ring off, the rustle of papers being collected, his feet in the corridor, slowing down, coming into the bar. He turned his back to the door and tipped down his rum and scowled at Maurits to hurry. Maurits grinned back affectionately.

'Come *on*' snapped Dell. He turned, passed quickly behind the tweedy journalist, out into the corridor — and stopped dead in consternation. Entering the hotel, bag in hand, gear slung round his neck was Mealy-head. There could be no mistaking the big glowering face and rolling gait. Dell backed into the bar and grabbed Maurits' arm, oblivious of the tweedy man. Maurits brightened, thinking it was a reprieve. Dell hissed, 'The church? You know the church, the big church. *Kirke!*' He pointed in the general direction.

Maurits nodded his head vigorously, then sunk it in an exaggerated attitude of prayer, rolling his eyes up so that only the blotchy whites showed.

'Good, good. In five minutes. *Funf minuten.*' He splayed out five fingers.

Maurits nodded again.

'Okay.' Dell peered down the corridor again. He couldn't see Mealy-head. He ventured a few steps. Mealy-head was at the reception desk, his back turned to the foyer. Dell slipped off his new coat, folded it and swung it over his shoulder to hide his face from one side, drew a deep breath and made a dash for the exit. Too late, he saw a fur-coated woman with a dog coming from the outside.

'Hey, you!' It was Mealy-head's voice.

Dell pushed past the woman, heard her dog yelp as he trod on its paw, smelled the moth-ball smell of her fur coat and was down the one step and walking hard, not running, towards the nearest market stalls, fifty yards away. Behind him he heard Mealy-head shouting at him again to come back, then the crowds enveloped him. He bent his head low and ducked between the stalls, past a crockery barker brandishing a fan of white plates, past the heaps of jumpers and cardigans, the lines of flapping dresses, rolls of lino and mounds of cut flowers, dodging and nudging people, calling out that he was sorry until he was opposite the bridge. At a stall spread with thumbed American magazines he paused and glanced backwards. There was no sign of pursuit. At the bridge he attached himself to a cluster of people waiting to cross the road. He didn't dare look back now but kept his face averted from the market place. There was a gap in the traffic and they crossed. Dell cut up the lane Harvey had taken the previous evening. He passed the fisherman's pub, an antique shop, a tiny café, then the lane opened out to a green lawn, flagged paths and the southern flank of the church. Dell stopped and swore under his breath.

Outside the massive oak doors were two more photographers. One of them had his camera slung round his neck, the other's rested on top of a bulky leather box on the ground by his feet. They were stamping their feet to keep warm; a thin plume of blue cigarette smoke streamed away in the wind. But they were looking towards the main approach to the church from the end of the market square, and a little further over ten or twelve women were also waiting: even as Dell watched there was a buzz of excitement among the women and the photographer whose camera was on the ground picked it up, and a black limousine with white fluttering ribbons came crunching up. The bride was arriving, and all attention was on her.

Dell walked unconcernedly across the grass, round the base of the tower to the north door on the other side of the church. Inside it was warmer and lighter than he'd expected. The bride, delayed by the photographers, was only just entering on the arm of a silver-haired man in morning dress who carried himself with exaggerated stiffness. Behind them the doors were closed again, the organ launched into its piece with a trill of high cold notes over a reverberating bass and the little huddle of wedding guests craned in their seats to watch their progress up the aisle.

Nancy and the children were on their own at the back of the seating. Dell trod carefully between the rows of seats and sat down beside them. Nancy was smiling sentimentally. 'It's nice, isn't it?' she said.

'What's nice?'

'The wedding, of course. What else?' She changed the subject. 'They didn't half give me a funny look when I sat

143

down with the baby and everything. Some young fellow wanted to know if I was a friend of the bride's or the bridegroom's. I said I'd known her in the Girl Guides and just wanted to look, you know. Anyway, I had to sit down. My arm was breaking with carrying the baby

'Listen,' Dell broke in. 'You're to go on the ship in a minute. There's someone coming who'll take you.'

'What about you?' The question bounced back.

'I've got to go on later.'

'I've had enough on my own. I'm not going anywhere more without you.'

'I'm sorry, sweetie. It's the last time.' He squeezed her hand and gave her a peck on the cheek, then the corner of her eye, tasting the salt of an incipient tear.

The congregation was scraping its chairs and struggling to its feet for a hymn. Nancy sniffed and fumbled for her hanky. She opened a gold-printed folder and found the words. 'The fellow gave us this,' she said.

Tony reached up. 'I want it. Can I have it, Mum?'

'Sssh. Go'n sit by your daddy.'

Tony pushed past her and hoisted himself on to the seat by Dell. The congregation sang its way thinly through the hymn, one woman's voice rising bossily above the others. The couple stood stiffly at the steps before the empty choir stalls, supported by a best man, a bridesmaid and a tiny boy in yellow satin who jiffled from one foot to another. The baby sat on Nancy's lap and played with the buttons on her coat. Dell kept an anxious look-out for Maurits.

'What's the matter?' whispered Nancy.

'Wondering where he's got to, the engineer who's taking you to the ship.'

'Don't fret. He'll turn up.'

The priest embarked on a prayer, his voice rising and falling in prayerful style. Tony said, 'What's that little boy in yellow for? Is it his birthday?' It reminded him of something. 'When we going to have the firewuks, Daddy? Is it today, Daddy, the firewuks?' His voice piped up higher and higher. A couple of heads in the rear of the congregation turned round disapprovingly and Dell saw a verger in black cassock staring their way. He clapped a silencing hand over Tony's mouth.

The ceremony progressed. The couple had advanced to the altar rails for the final part of the service and the little page in yellow had been seized by a protective woman in a too tight tweed costume before there was a minor explosion from the entrance and Maurits came blundering in, his red face owlish, his woollen hat still on his head. He carried a bunch of carnations. The verger was already advancing on him. Dell slipped from his seat and beckoned. Maurits ignored the verger and steered uneasily for Dell.

'Allo,' he said.

'Hat!' hissed Dell, pointing. 'Your hat.'

Maurits felt to see what had happened to his hat, rolling his eyes like a juggler with a couple of eggs.

'*Off!*'

Maurits clawed it off. Three or four isolated strands of black hair curled from the top of his head; otherwise he was bald. The aroma of rum hung thickly around him.

'How many more did you have, for God's sake?' demanded Dell. He led him to where Nancy and the kids were sitting. Up at the altar rails the priest had gone into the benediction and even the usual nervous coughing of the wedding party was stilled. Maurits hiccupped, and blundering along the line of chairs managed to make each one rasp on the floor. Nancy greeted him eyes bulging with doubt. Maurits bestowed the flowers on her, made an ineffectual grab for her hand and noticing the baby wetly kissed the top of its head. The baby's face went bright red and crumpled as she organised an outraged bellow. Heads turned all over the church. The verger jumped as if shot. '*Sssh, sssh*' implored Nancy.

Music came to the rescue, a spirited voluntary while the bride and groom and a contingent of witnesses filed into the vestry to sign the register. 'Listen to the pretty music,' urged Nancy jogging the baby in time to it. The baby looked up to the high painted ceiling trying to see where the sound came from. She sobbed deeply, then again and again, but the sobs getting progressively slighter.

Maurits leaned towards Dell exhaling rummy fumes. 'The man with camera,' he said. He imitated holding a camera up to his eye and wiggled his forefinger up and down on an imaginary button. 'Very uh … *viel bose* with you.' He stabbed the forefinger in Dell's breast. 'Wa-wa-wa-wa-wa-wa.' That was supposed to be the sound of shouting.

'Where?' Dell was alarmed.

Maurits pointed to the doors.

Dell shook his head. 'No, it's another man. He's not cross.'

Maurits nodded his head emphatically. He pointed to himself. 'I see him.'

'Stay there a minute, then.' Dell slipped from his seat and cautiously let himself out by the north door. Bright sun met him. He worked his way back round the tower. There was a little side-chapel which hid the south porch from him. He had to edge his way uncomfortably near before he saw them. Mealy-head was talking to one of the wedding photographers, pointing back down the little lane, then towards the market place — Dell noticed the line of waiting wedding cars — finally past the other man's nose at the church itself. Behind him were the tweed-suited reporter who'd been in the hotel and another photographer, an older man in a black homburg hat. Dell hastily retreated the way he'd come.

There was a cough, a faint nervous laugh from the vestry: the verger began elaborately to open the great doors and the air in the church quivered as the organ blared the deep preliminary notes of the Wedding March. From the vestry door the bride appeared, veil thrown back, the groom self-consciously at her side.

'Where've they been?' said Tony. 'What's been happening?'

'They're married now,' said Nancy.

All eyes were on the couple. 'Come on, come on,' urged Dell. He shepherded everyone towards the north door and going ahead of them opened it a crack and took a precautionary peep out. He flinched. Homburg hat and tweed-suit had moved round from the main entrance and taken up stations just outside. Dell closed the crack and looked anxiously over his shoulder. The south doors were now wide open, the bride and groom standing in the tall Gothic aperture to be photographed.

'Quickly!' He chivvied Nancy, the children, Maurits, to the rear of the nave, between tall painted gates into a high vaulted chamber. The walls bore plaques and were hung with photographs. They were under the tower, and at least hidden from anyone peering into the church from outside.

Nancy said, 'What's the matter?'

'Trouble,' said Dell briefly. 'You've got to become wedding guests.' He looked at Maurits. 'Though how, I don't know.' He jerked Maurits' jacket trying to smooth the wrinkles, turned the collar down, pulled his tie straight, confiscated the woolly hat from his side pocket. Maurits still looked a mess. He had an idea and slipped off his new overcoat and Maurits wriggled into it. It came down below his knees but he looked much better.

'Here, give him one of these,' said Nancy. She broke off a carnation head from the bunch.

Dell threaded it into Maurits' buttonhole. With the overcoat unbuttoned it looked quite effective. Maurits sniffed it and went into pantomimes of extravagant pleasure.

'Hair,' said Dell, pointing.

Maurits licked the palm of his hand and smeared the wisps of hair flat on his head.

'You'll do.' He turned his attention to the others. Tony looked quite neat. Nancy had already pinned three more of the carnations on to her coat. They made a surprising difference. Dell heard whispers of commotion. 'Oh God, what next?'

Maurits had strayed away and attached himself to the wedding group, now swollen to include a dozen or more relatives and hangers-on. The photographers were using flashes as the sun became screened by the porch. Maurits was standing in pompous mock-Napoleonic attitude at one end of the line. A tall woman in a hat like a land-mine turned an astonished greyhound profile on him. The silvery man in morning dress moved across and said something, taking him by the sleeve. Maurits wrenched his arm away, and gave the man in morning dress a playful push. The ever-watchful verger took a step toward the scene. The man's face darkened. Dell could see his lips mouthing the words 'Now look here —' He groaned to Nancy, 'We get an accomplice and he has to be a drunk.'

'I can handle him. I handled enough like him when I was behind the bar.' She looked at Dell with confident grey eyes.

'I believe you could, but be careful. Avoid any more of a scene than there is already. The baby's a bit incongruous but there's

148

nothing we can do about it. Just look as if you couldn't find a baby minder.' He looked at her. 'You ought to have a hat, though.'

She held up Maurits' woolly cap with a grimace.

'I'll buy you a shampoo.'

She grinned and pulled the hat on. It covered her head like a bag. She pulled it off, shook her hair, rolled the hem of the hat up and tried again. With a bit of kneading it looked almost becoming. Dell put his head on one side. 'Suits you,' he glanced up just in time to see the little yellow page duck from under Maurits' reach and hear his yelp of distress. He kissed her. 'It'll be all right, love. You see. It'll be all right.' She held her head against his chest for a second, then picked up the baby and was gone.

Something warned Dell not to watch her. He looked the other way. Tweed-suit and the Homburg hat were pushing their way in through the north door. Tweed-suit shouted, 'There he is!'

Dell took four, five, six quick paces to a little pointed door not two feet wide set inconspicuously in the masonry of the tower. He lifted the old iron latch and slipped through without looking back.

He found himself on the first stone step of a spiral staircase that wound tightly upwards. The only hand-rail was a thick rope held by iron rings fixed to the wall every six feet or so. Electric wall lights cast an intermittent illumination. As he climbed he found his path tending to stray inwards, where the triangular steps narrowed to vanishing point. Twice he stubbed his toe. It seemed he climbed for ten minutes before he reached daylight streaming through a doorway, but it was probably much less. He stepped out on a stone platform. The air penetrated his clothes and made icy cold a trickle of sweat running down his side from the exertions of the climb. He inhaled deeply and looked over the breast-high parapet. Below him was the great upturned slate keel of the main roof, beyond it the still crowded market place. He moved to where he could see the lower roof of the flanking chapel and stuck on to it, as if by a child with a building set, the block of the entrance porch. Dinky toy limousines inched as close as they could and took on antlike wedding guests. He spotted Nancy and the others. Maurits was making some sort of flamboyant signal. In answer to it the last of the wedding cars crawled up and Maurits had the door open for Nancy.

'Good for you, friend,' said Dell. The wind whipped away his words. 'But keep away from the reception.' He examined the scene further. Of Mealy-head there was no sign. He withdrew from the parapet and took his immediate bearings, marching briskly round the four sides of the platform. In addition to the staircase he had ascended there was another at the next corner. He put his head through the aperture and listened carefully: down in the depths there seemed to be something, a bump, the scrape of iron on stone, a sound that might have been heavy breathing. He went back to the first one and tried that: a murmur, and suddenly, quite clearly funnelling up the narrow tube of the shaft, a voice: 'How much bloody higher do we go then?'

Dell fought down a spasm of panic and transferred to the other side of the tower. He discovered that although there were only two staircases thus far, there were four — one at each corner — continuing upwards. He chose the nearest and began to climb. In a moment he was in total darkness; there were no wall lamps now, nor the comfort of the guide rope. Once a tiny glazed slot in the enclosing walls admitted a pool of light then blackness reasserted itself. The wind outside was a steady roar. The rotating upwards motion began to have a hypnotic effect. At last another brighter radiance signalled the top. He was panting now. The wind reached in his open mouth and struck at the sweat round his waistband and made listening down the shafts almost impossible. He was on the top of the main, square tower but a slender octagonal lantern tower rose another forty or fifty feet. He hunted for a door into it, found one; it was locked. He hurried back to his staircase. The steps continued upwards inside the stone pinnacle which crowned each corner of the tower. A wooden barrier closed them off at waist height, with a notice saying danger — no admittance. Dell ducked underneath and crept up. The staircase made a last turn and a half and then simply converged into the fabric of the pinnacle. He sat down on the last step wide enough to take him and waited. He found another little slot, this time unglazed, which gave a view of part of the top of the tower.

In an unnervingly short time there was the sound of footsteps but no one at first came into Dell's narrow wedge of vision. Then there were further footsteps and breathless greetings. Mealy-head puffed into view. 'Christ,' he said, 'it's parky up here.'

A voice Dell recognised as the tweedy reporter's said something he couldn't catch. The man seemed to be carrying out a systematic inspection of the top of the tower. The heavy tread of his feet would be followed by a moment's quiet, then on he went again. After a couple of minutes the voice came more clearly. 'There's another tower that goes up higher, but I don't see how he could have got in without a key.'

'He never came up here,' said Mealy-head. 'I told you he would never come up here. That old verger was having you on.'

'We saw him. We bloody well saw him. I should know.'

'Well, he nipped down again as we were coming up.'

151

'He couldn't have. Ernie and that local stringer fellow took the other stairs. There were only two lots up to the first stage.' There was a pause, then: 'I say, the steps go on up into these little spires. Maybe he's hidden in one of them.'

'Yeah, sure. Him and the brigade of guards.'

'Seriously. I'm going to have a look.'

Dell tensed himself for despairing action. Then from immediately below came a fresh sound of laboured breathing. Someone was ascending the staircase beneath him.

'*Ernie!*' It was Mealy-head's voice. 'You shouldn't have come up here. There was no need.' He sounded concerned.

The homburg-hatted photographer staggered into Dell's view. He would have been distinguished-looking if his grey hair hadn't been straggling damply from below the homburg brim and his face whey-coloured from exertion. He was mopping the corners of his mouth with a handkerchief and he sounded as if he were going to be sick.

Dell heard Tweed-suit, 'All right, all right, old boy. Now take it easy. Head down and big breaths.' He seemed to have forgotten about his little spires. Presently Homburg-Hat began to recover. 'Phew,' he said weakly. 'Never do that again. I thought I was going to pass out half-way up, there in the dark and the steepness.'

Mealy-head must have been looking over the parapet. 'What a view! You could do some interesting stuff from here with the right lens and an hour to spare.'

'Too hazy.'

'Not with the right gear.'

Dell felt his right leg starting to deaden as the edge of the step cut into his circulation. He forced himself to stay utterly still. The man in the homburg hat moved out of vision. Dell tried to shift his weight slightly. The deadened muscles gave and he nearly toppled. His hand slipped on the slimy stone, then held with a stinging pain in the fingertips. He held his mouth wide open to still his breathing but the sound of his heart seemed to fill the air. Perhaps two seconds of silence passed. Then Mealy-head's sounded again.

'You can see forty miles, I shouldn't wonder.'

'Maybe,' said Tweed-suit. 'But it's cold. It's getting dark and I should think we're being scooped all over the shop by the others. Come on, Ernie.' Mealy-head followed, mumbling after them. 'Scooped, you say? There won't be any scoops the way the town's filling up with blokes. The *Pic's* got five here, I'm told. All the Saturday only boys. It's the first out of town job they've had for months…' His voice tailed off in the concentration of descending the narrow stairs. Dell listened to the scraping of feet and muffled curses and the bumping of Mealy-head's camera satchel against the stone walls until it had dwindled to nothing. Then at last he lowered himself from his perch and down the five, six, seven steps out into the open again and stamped around screwing his features in pain until the pins and needles in his leg became bearable again.

He crossed to the parapet and considered the view that Mealy-head had wanted to photograph. The roofs of the town spread all around in a jumble of different angles, planes, colours — red tile, grey slate, iron corrugated, some rectangular and precise, others dipping and curving with age. On the ridge of the canning factory three enormous chimney cowls swung to and fro in perfect time. Beyond the town the flat fen landscape stretched away drably in the fading light, criss-crossed by drainage ditches, roads, hedges, all as rectilinear as the grid lines on an ordnance map. Even the olive-green river ran a straight course except for its undulations through the town. Dell studied it carefully. Immediately below him it flowed past the little lawn and tawny paths and bushy trees of the church precinct; then behind the lane with the fisherman's pub — he could even see the dinghy moored by the steps; under the town bridge, reflecting the lights that were beginning to come on; then through a ragged S-bend and under the Swing Bridge before making its big loop round the docks. Dell identified the Riverside Wharf, the warehouse, the dusty white shed of the fertiliser company, but the *Posy* herself was masked by the high sea wall. Even the river channel here was out of sight except for the glistening mud bank of the far shore. Beyond the mud was flat grass-grown tideland, then a low dyke and an electricity transformer station, a complex of strange shapes in a high-fenced enclosure joined by swooping cables to the line of pylons that strode across the landscape from the south.

Dell shivered and turned his jacket collar up. He stamped round the tower banging his feet to try and get warm. To the west the sun had dipped below the horizon haze but its last rays caught the vapour trail of a distant jet and turned it bright gold. Nearer at hand the lights of town were still going on steadily, one here, two there, then a whole street, but always at a uniform rate as if people were consciously obeying some statistical law. Suddenly something hissed up from the dusk, a puny thing that burned out before it rose to half Dell's altitude: for the first time he was seeing a rocket from above. Down in the lane at the foot of the church there was a sharp bang of a cracker and a boy's exaggerated, formal laugh. Towards the docks a bonfire flickered into life. Somewhere a clock began the business of striking the hour. Another took it up, then the church clock itself, deep down in the fabric of the tower. Dell stepped into the nearest pinnacle and began the long, careful descent.

As he neared the bottom a notice warned him to be quiet — every sound could be heard in the church. At the bottom he paused for a moment before carefully lifting the latch. The church was lighted but almost empty. One family walked slowly up a side aisle, their heels ringing on the stone flags, a little girl in a white fur hat lagging behind. They all stopped to look at a plaque on the wall. The father pointed and Dell heard his voice droning something, and a child's voice saying clearly, 'Who was he, Daddy, and why did he fight?'

Dell stepped into the church and began to close the door. Someone had been standing behind it, in his blind spot, someone clearing his throat to speak … Dell braced himself to run. The door closed. It was the verger, but now without his cassock, just a pleasant little man in a grey herring-bone suit. He said, 'That'll be a shilling please.'

'What?'

'For going up the tower, sir.'

'Oh yes. I'm sorry. I didn't see you…' Dell fumbled in his pocket for his change. Two coins tinkled to the floor and rolled away. The verger stooped down and retrieved a penny, and looked carefully for the other one, putting his hands on his knees and bending stiffly and frowning down at the shadows made by chairs and a table on which were arrayed pamphlets and postcards. 'It doesn't matter,' said Dell. 'It wasn't much.'

'It sounded like silver,' said the verger. He seemed quite concerned.

Dell found a half-crown. 'Honestly, it doesn't matter. Here's what I owe you.'

The verger began to feel in his pocket. Dell said, 'Keep the change. I mean, put it in the maintenance box or something.'

'That's very good of you,' said the verger. He smiled.

He opened his mouth to say something, changed his mind and hurried away with a 'Good night.' When he got into the cold air outside he found he had to blink.

There was something different about the town, an air of tension that Dell noticed at once and didn't much like. In the market place the stallholders had begun to pack their stuff away but the crowds still hung about, as if waiting for something. The white-coated evening paper sellers were busy, with fluttering contents bills that said MISSING SCIENTIST IN BOSTON? as well as HALF-TIME SCORES. The spasmodic banging of fireworks or sudden hiss of a rocket added to the jumpiness.

Dell found he was cold and hungry. He had hardly eaten all day. He tramped around uncertainly and eventually found a nondescript fish and chip shop in a side street. He sat at a little plastic-topped table trying to chew his way through a piece of cod and a heap of chips but a mounting uneasiness made him leave half of it, and hurry back to the square. A newspaper van was dumping a fresh bundle of papers with one of the vendors. Dell joined a little queue which formed immediately and bought a copy, ostentatiously turning to the sports results in the stop-press panel. He stopped by a coal office and grimly examined the front page picture which had caught his eye. It was one of the ones Mealy-head had snatched at the works that day — his office must have decided to release it before Sunday. Luckily the likeness wasn't very good. He'd been shouting and the mouth was an odd square shape. The rest of the face, enlarged, grainy, devoid of shading, didn't look too much like the one reflected back to Dell from the coal office window, but he had an idea and bought a cap to pull down over his eyes from a market stall.

Over an hour remained before the time the skipper had stipulated. The lights of a cinema attracted him and he bought a ticket for the cheapest part and sat in the warm darkness for half an hour watching a succession of advertising filmlets and the start of the second feature, until a sudden resurgence of anxiety drove him out again. The other side of the market place lines of people waited for the country buses. He hurried across; one was just pulling away that would do. He swung himself aboard as it slowed to turn over the Town Bridge.

The conductor frowned. 'That's how people get hurt,' he said reprovingly.

'Sorry.'

The bus jerked to a stop, held up by the traffic lights beyond the bridge. A policeman stood on the pavement. A sergeant and an inspector were talking to him. The inspector was a bull-like man. Dell could see the back of his neck bulging over his hard white collar. He wore a long stiff mackintosh with two silver stars on the shoulder straps and as Dell watched gestured with a heavy black cane, pointing first to the market place then across the bridge. As the bus began to move again he tucked it crisply under his arm and turned away, gloved hand rising in answer to the policeman's salute. The sergeant followed him.

The conductor was jingling his bag of change. Dell hesitated to specify the Swing Bridge, asked instead for the housing estate where Stella lived. The bus ground along the High Street, past the square bulk of the cannery, over the little level crossing and past the Swing Bridge. Dell forced himself to stay in his seat. Some figures were busy in a patch of wasteland. Dell heard their cries and the flash of a torch beam. He dropped off at the next stop but one, crossed the road and doubled back in the shadows of a high brick wall. When the bus was out of sight behind him he recrossed the road and made for the bridge. The sound of the children calling beckoned him. There was the flare of a match being struck, and a moment later the flicker of growing flames. The children cheered excitedly. It was their bonfire. There were ten or eleven of them, and a grown-up man with muffler wound round his neck who was urging them to stand back. A woman stood a little way away, holding up a tiny child on her shoulder. As Dell drew level there was more shrill excitement as a firework fizzed a spray of golden sparks into the air, followed by a sharper, shorter fizz and a bang. Dell slowed up and bit his lip. He heard the grown-up shouting, 'One at a time, one at a time. Or they'll all be gone, you sillies!'

Dell was near the bridge now. He could see the keeper in his little round box. He took two irresolute steps, and peered through the dark for the distant, high swaying light that marked the position of the *Posy*. Among the groups of children was a sudden quietness, broken as a more elaborate firework began to toss up balls of fire which wriggled and crackled in all directions.

'Oh hell, oh bloody hell,' said Dell to himself, quite loudly. He took a step backwards, hesitated again, then retraced his steps past the kids and the adult in his muffler who was crying, 'Now keep back boys keep back, or someone will get *burned*,' past the woman with the child on her shoulder. He was looking for the lights of a shop. A garage clock indicated 5.50. He dropped back into a walk, his breath steaming in the air.

At last he came to a narrow lane which had been chopped in half like a worm by the main road. It curled away on each side into the flat wet countryside. A hundred yards down the lane was a single wavery street light, a pillar box and the yellow glow of a window. Dell found himself running again. A bell clanged stiffly as he pushed the door open. A woman behind the counter was serving a woman customer with biscuits. 'It's not right,' she was saying. 'I mean, it's not as if it were her fault she had to go to the hospital, is it? It's not a crime to have them things growing in you.'

The woman customer made a *tsk-tsk* in agreement 'I don't know, I'm sure,' she said.

Dell jiffled his feet and sighed.

'Was there something?' said the shop woman.

'Fireworks,' said Dell. 'Any fireworks left?'

'In the back room there, we had them. I don't know what's left. Not much, I shouldn't think, but you're welcome to have a look. I'll put the light on.' She fumbled behind a calendar on the wall and the light went on in an inner room. It was really only a storeroom, a table had been set up and fireworks were displayed in cardboard boxes on it.

'Anything you fancy?' said the woman.

'Oh, some,' said Dell. 'These. I can't decide about any others. I don't know what he'd like…' He heard the panicky tone to his voice.

'There should be one or two boxes up on the shelf there. You know, the five-shilling assortment.'

'That would be just the thing,' said Dell. He found the boxes and grabbed one.

'Doesn't have any bangers, that's the only thing. Is it a little boy?'

'Yes. It doesn't matter, though,' said Dell hurriedly. He pulled out his pocketful of change. There was just enough. The woman put the little box in a paper bag and the shop bell clanged again behind him. He ran along the lane, really running now, his feet landing mushily on dead leaves. At the garage the clock stood at five past six. He lapsed into a fast walk. Then he let out a howl of despair. The Swing Bridge was moving —

pivoting slowly round on a central pier, the ends already well clear of the banks. Dell hurled himself forward, crossing the road in a long slant heedless of the traffic, oblivious of the kids and their bonfire. As he reached the grass bank the bridge had come to rest along the length of the river, marooned on its island pier. Dell sank to his knees in rage and mortification. The cold, wet earth striking through his trousers brought him to his senses. He made for the little signal box and hammered on the door.

'Who is it?' The man who opened the door was pulling a fawn mackintosh on over his railway uniform.

'Is the bridge going to be closed for long?'

'Till Monday morning.'

'*What?*'

'No trains into the docks on a Sunday, mate. Nothing doing there.' He started to put out the lights in the box.

'You couldn't open it again…?'

'You're dead right I couldn't. You'll have to go round, mate.' He closed the door behind him and locked it. Seeing Dell's distress, he added more kindly, 'I'm sorry, but in any case the smacks are going out. We'd have to wait a good half-hour to let 'em through. You'd be as quick going round.'

Dell muttered some thanks and set off towards the town. Passing a brick wall he banged his fist against it until his knuckles smarted and putting them to his mouth he tasted blood. The only way into the docks now was by the main entrance, all the way to the market place and out again the other side. He kept a watch over his shoulder to see if a bus were coming and once tentatively thumbed a lorry that thundered past. His feet were getting sore from his comings and goings over hard roads. A brainwave struck him and he

160

veered left towards the railway and picked up a taxi in the station yard.

At the Town Bridge the policeman had been joined by another in a flat cap and an old-fashioned button-up tunic. The taxi seemed to glide along. As they approached the docks Dell looked anxiously ahead. There seemed to be a lot of lights, one of them blue and winking … a little delivery van in front of the taxi slowed down, the driver signalling he was going to stop.

'What's a matter with him,' grumbled the taxi driver. The van stopped. In front of it was a third vehicle, also stationary. Someone came forward to speak to the van driver. It looked like the inspector Dell had noticed from the bus earlier on. There were more uniforms in the background and the parked police car whose blue roof light was flashing on and off…

The taxi was pulling up. Dell leaned forward. 'Can you cut through to the left,' he said urgently. 'It's — er, that place over there I want.' He pointed to an institutional looking building adjacent to the dock area and reached by a side turning.

'The old men's home, you mean? You said the docks.' But he started to pull over.

'No, sorry, the dock *road*, I said. I meant the home.'

The taxi inched past the rear of the van. A dock policeman held up his hand. The taxi driver pointed to the old men's home and the policeman stood aside and waved them through.

'Visiting hour, is it?' asked the driver.

'Yes. It's the old fella. He's not too good.'

'Ah, I'm sorry to hear that. It's the time of the year, I dare say. Here we are.'

Dell had no change. He dug out a note from the wallet he kept buttoned down in his trouser pocket. He noticed the driver staring at his torn knuckles and the box of fireworks still clutched in his hand. 'Take five bob,' he said hurriedly.

He stood in front of the entrance putting his wallet away and pretending to ring the doorbell while the taxi laboriously turned round and at last drove off. He waited until its tail lights turned out of sight and hastened after it on foot. The policemen and police car were still stationed in front of the docks and at the moment they had no vehicles waiting to go in. Dell had no time to hesitate. He marched firmly past on the other side of the road, whistling a tune of sorts, examining the fireworks box in his hand as if it were some important packet he had to deliver in the town. No shout, no summons came. For the second time that day sweat trickled coldly down his side.

The market place was nearly empty now. The uprights of the last stall were being heaved with a clatter on to the roof rack of a battered limousine. Outside the hotel six or seven cars were parked, among them Hunter's. There was also a television van. 'I'll give you sods a story yet,' Dell promised them. He was very calm now. He stepped for a moment into the doorway of a closed shop to straighten his tie and comb his hair.

The Fisherman's pub was nearly empty. Only a couple of market stallholders gripped pint glasses in mittened hands. Dell frowned. He needed a busy houseful really. 'Not many in tonight?' he said.
'Early yet,' said the big publican without looking up. He was checking a football coupon against the evening paper. A pair of scholarly horn-rims rested on his prize-fighter's nose. Dell ordered a rum. The publican reached for a glass, jammed it under the optic dispenser and pushed it towards Dell without lifting his eyes from his coupon. 'Two and three,' he said tonelessly.

The clock with the tobacco dial suggested 6.35. Allowing for pub-time it was probably ten minutes earlier. Three more men came in. One addressed by the others as Charlie was full of the big excitement. 'They reckon the Peacock's stiff with reporter fellows, and the telly too, not to mention twice as many police out than's usual when there's no home game, specials and all!'

'They're stopping cars at the Town Bridge even,' one of the others added.

'What is it then? Do they reckon he's trying to get on a ship?'

'That's what I heard,' said Charlie. He had a thin neck and little birdy eyes but a big nose, so he looked a bit like an ostrich. 'There's seven going out on the tide, so he'd have a choice. He'd have a choice, eh?'

'When is the tide?' asked Dell diffidently.

They looked at him. 'Seven-thirty,' said Charlie.

Dell drank off his rum and slid the glass towards the publican. 'I'll have another rum, please, a double.' He tapped the money on the bar.

'All right, I heard you.'

Dell drank most of it in one swig. It was perhaps a mistake. The others looked at him again. The spirit burned its way down. His knees were trembling. He waited while Charlie embarked on a story about a dog, waited for the laughter at the end, and as Charlie repeated the punch-line — 'He said 'That's not a Basset hound, that's a bloody Bassett's all-sort" — he walked nonchalantly out to the little courtyard and opened the green urinal door with the three ventilation holes and let it go. By the time it closed on its spring he'd opened a gate in the iron railing and was halfway down the stone steps, pulling at the stiff, cold rope that held the dinghy. He'd got one foot in, feeling for the bottom, other foot taking the weight, when he remembered about oars. There was nothing in the boat itself.

His eyes scanned the little yard: dustbin, tub with dead plants, a crate of empty bottles. The crate was the only possibility. He went back two steps and he could reach it. He lugged it towards him and began to take out the bottles, carefully putting them down one by one. After the first half-dozen impatience took over. Two bottles clinked together, another fell over and rolled round in a semi-circle till it fetched up against the railing. Dell upturned the crate and let the remaining bottles fall into the water with a splash and slowly sink. Back in the dinghy, he jerked at the painter, trying to undo the knot that secured it to the ring in the wall. Suddenly he froze. The door from the tap room opened with a bang and a figure strode into the yard. A cigarette end traced a parabola of light and landed in the water with a hiss. The man went into the Gents. Dell dropped on to his heels in the swaying boat.

He heard the man whistling tunelessly and clearing his throat and hawking, then the door banging open again and retreating footsteps. He hooked his fingers in the rope and this time the knot unslipped. He shoved the dinghy away from the wall, sat down unsteadily in the stern and took up the crate. It made an impossibly awkward paddle; if he dug the open side into the water it braked and twisted in his hands; when he pulled it out water cascaded on to his legs. The stern swung an inch or two, but the bow didn't seem to move at all. Dell reversed the crate, gripping the edges with fingers already chilled. The dinghy lurched a few inches crabwise. He lifted the dripping crate out and tried smashing it against the gunwale. The sound was loud, the crate stood fast. Dell perceived that a gentle current had taken the dinghy, moving it back into the river wall. He swore and reached out to control the impact. There was the sound of the pub's yard door opening again and a giant figure loomed overhead.

'And what the bloody hell do you think you're doing?' demanded the publican.

'Just going for a little fishing,' said Dell in a stage drunk's accent.

'What's going on, then?' Charlie had followed the publican out.

'Wanna catch some fish,' Dell supplemented. Even dinning in his own ears the voice sounded thin and implausible.

'Here, give us a hand,' said the publican to Charlie. With Charlie holding on to his outstretched hand, he came down the steps to the last slimy one lapped by the water. He leaned out a long leg, hooked his foot over the dinghy's gunwale and pulled it in. 'Come on out, you,' he said.

Dell stumbled on to the steps, saying, 'Sure, sure, sure,' in his thin drunken voice, managing a strained giggle as he pretended to slip and nearly fall. Next minute he felt the publican's hand close on his arm like a clamp. The big sergeant-major's face was thrust close to his.

'I thought it must be you,' he said, 'Hey, Charlie, see he doesn't get away while I fix the dinghy.' The iron grip relaxed, Dell tried another giggle and looked at Charlie.

'You heard what he said,' said Charlie anxiously.

'Indeed I did,' said Dell, switching to drunks-type gravity. 'There's no need for you to worry. I shall explain everything — everything — to mine hosht here.'

'Yeah? We'll see about that,' said the publican. He trod purposefully up the steps.

'It was only a joke.'

'Was it?'

'Of course.' He dropped the drunk act.

'That's better. No one gets taken like that on three tots of rum.'

'Not on your tots, Alf,' said Charlie. He laughed. 'Not on your tots.'

Dell was briefly grateful to him. The publican snorted and led Dell under the light on the wall outside the urinal and peered at him again. He fumbled for his glasses. Dell could smell the tobacco-wet-sheep smell of his tweed jacket. 'You aren't this individual they're looking for, are you?'

'What individual?'

'This secret agent or whatever it is? They were talking about him just now.'

'Do I look like a secret agent? It was a joke. I saw the boat and had an impulse to get in it...' Dell was aware he was shivering, trembling all over.

Light and noise spilled from the pub as someone else came out to the Gents. 'Aye, aye,' he said. 'What's this? a branch meeting?'

'Trying to take the dinghy, he was,' said Charlie.

The publican said, 'All right, Charlie, save your stories for later. I'll ring the coppers.' But he stayed where he was, frowning down at Dell.

'Had a drop too many?' asked the newcomer.

'Only three rums, said Charlie. I said to Alf, it would take more'n three of his tots to do the trick.' He laughed louder than ever. 'Not on your tots, Alf,' I said.

'Shut up,' said the publican. 'It could be that agent or whoever it is they reckon they're looking for. Are those coppers still at Town Bridge?'

'They were ten minutes ago,' said Charlie. 'I saw them.'

'Nip up and fetch one,' the publican said to the man who'd just come out.

'If you like.' He looked wistfully at the green door with the three ventilator holes drilled in it. 'I was just going to go in there.'

'When you get back,' said the publican. 'When you get back.' He took hold of Dell's arm again. 'You're coming back inside with us. Just sit there quiet and finish your drink, you understand? No fuss, no trouble, that's how it's going to be. If you start anything, I'll make it bad for you. Understand?'

'Whatever you say.' Dell had got the trembling under control but his legs were still weak. He looked unbelievingly at the tweedy bulk of the innkeeper and past him at the withered plant in its tub.

'And that goes for you, too, Charlie,' added the innkeeper. 'You can belt up and all.'

They filed back into the pub. There were five or six others in it now and a woman serving behind the little bar. She looked at them curiously, the others didn't take much notice. The man who'd emerged last said, 'See you,' and went briskly on his way out to the street.

Dell's glass was still on the bar. The publican pushed it across the bar to have another tot added, and handed it to him. 'You look as if you could do with this.'

'That's kind of you.' He drank it down. 'I'm very sorry for behaving so stupidly —'

'You won't get round me. I'll give you a drink — I'd give any a drink who was shaking like you. But you'll not get me to change my mind, so you might as well save your breath.'

'It was only for a sort of stunt,' said Dell. 'You see, I'm a journalist. I was trying to find out just how easy it would be to escape from this town…'

'Yeah, and I'm Shirley Temple.'

'He sounds like a journalist, I'll admit.' It was Charlie.

'I can prove it,' said Dell. 'You can ring up one of my colleagues at the hotel. Ask him to come over.'

'Nothing doing,' said the publican. 'Now just stay there quietly until the coppers get here.'

'It wouldn't do no harm to ring,' said Charlie. 'You don't want to look foolish, Alf.'

'I'd look a sight more foolish if I let him go now.' But Dell saw him glancing anxiously at the door and at the fast filling tap room.

'Are you going to give us a hand?' said the woman behind the bar. 'It's Saturday night, you know.'

'Yeah, all right.' The publican lifted a flap and let himself through. He turned to Dell. 'What would this fellow's name be?'

'Hunter. Bob Hunter.'

'And his paper?'

Dell told him.

He disappeared into an inner sanctum and Dell heard him dialling and then asking for Hunter.

'Fred is a long time fetching the police,' said Charlie conversationally.

'Yes,' said Dell absently. He was listening.

'No, *Hunter*, with a haitch … he's not … oh, he *is* … right you are.' The publican's beefy voice could have carried to the hotel without telephone wires. Then he was evidently talking to Hunter. He rang off and re-emerged. 'Mind you, it doesn't mean I've changed my mind,' he said defensively.

Dell nodded mutely. The next five minutes passed in an agony of suspense. Three times the street door opened; each time it was an ordinary customer; no police, no Hunter. The old tobacco-coloured clock ticked on to ten past seven and the church clock struck the hour.

The door opened a fourth time. Dell hardly dare look.

'Hullo, old boy. What have you been up to?'

Dell's mouth worked but he couldn't say anything. He heard the publican's voice as he bent over and spoke confidentially to Hunter. 'Do you know this man, sir?'

'Of course I know him. What is it? — Scotch?'

'Rum, I was drinking.'

'A rum and a Scotch.'

The publican said, 'I don't think you understand. I'm detaining this person while the police are fetched.'

'Why?'

'Because he was trying to steal my boat, that's why.'

'It was just for a lark,' said Dell.

'You ought to curb your sense of fun,' said Hunter. To the publican, 'He's always doing this kind of thing. Went for a swim in the fountains at Trafalgar Square once. Borrowed an electric milk float in the Isle of Wight. He's an embarrassment to us all.'

'That may be so,' said the publican heavily. 'This time he's unlucky. I've warned him, any messing about and I'll thump him. This is a decent house and I've got my licence to think about. I want no fuss.'

'Well, thumping people is hardly the way to go about it,' said Hunter. 'Now be a good chap and give us those drinks.'

Dell whispered, 'I must get away. They'll be back with the policeman any minute.'

'Have patience. He's wondering very hard if he's not made a fool of himself.'

The publican put the drinks on the bar. 'That'll be four-and-nine.' He hesitated and then said to Hunter, 'You can take your friend away. I don't want to see him again.'

Dell started the most heartfelt thank-you of his life. Hunter cut him off. 'Get going,' he snapped. 'The car's outside. I'll square up and follow you.'

Dell went. The street door seemed to lurch towards him. The policeman was just arriving, pushing importantly ahead of the man who'd gone to fetch him. He was another special. Dell saw a flat hat surmounting a long sorrowful face like a sheep's. It was too late to do anything but plunge blindly past him and run. He heard a confusion of shouts and then he was into a side alley which led direct into the market place. Instinctively he headed north, away from the pub, away from the docks, away from all the danger zones. He heard a horn toot and a car pulled into the kerb with a hiss from the tires. Dell had the door open and was manoeuvring himself into the passenger seat before it could come to a stop. Hunter let out the clutch, cursed as the engine juddered, rasped into first gear and accelerated.

'Blimey, you do things the hard way. Where to?'

'Straight on. There's a bridge somewhere round here called the Sluice Bridge. It's the only way left over the river, now, unless the coppers are there as well.'

'Could be,' said Hunter. 'The town's alive with them. There must be nearly as many coppers as there are reporters.' He squinted in his rear view mirror. 'The joke is, they none of them know what they're doing or who they're looking for.'

'Me.'

'Not really. No one's actually said you're wanted. It's a sort of self-generating witch-hunt. People join in because they're afraid not to. The reporters are afraid of being beaten. The police are afraid that someone's going to say you got away from here and they'll look silly. No one that I can think of really wants to stop you, they just daren't let you go.'

'Turn left at the next crossing,' said Dell. He was curiously passive; the reaction was too much. He slumped back in his seat with unfocused eyes, seeing street lights, patches of sky the colour of gun metal and cloud that looked like smoke the yellow flashes of Hunter's indicators reflected in upper windows. There was a policeman by the bridge, helmeted, sitting astride a motorcycle. But he was talking into a radio telephone handset, and took no notice as Hunter drove past. Dell saw him nodding into the angular handset as if whoever he was talking to could see him. Then they were passing ornamental copper globes and hearing the roar of the water pouring through the sluices.

'You see,' said Hunter. 'Nothing to it. Where now?' Next moment he cursed and braked. Almost before the road regained dry land it was barred by level crossing gates. The red lantern glowed stolidly. Behind them the motorcycle policeman was still talking into his phone.

'It's not as if there's anything going by,' said Hunter. 'They've just got the gates shut for fun.'

'I thought it was too good to be true.'

'You could nip out and cross by the pedestrian gate. I'll pick you up again as soon as I get over.' Before Dell could unlatch the door he whispered, 'Too late. He's coming this way. Get on the floor. Keep low.' Dell pushed his bottom forward and squeezed himself down in to the narrow well between his seat and the front bulkhead of the car. 'Head further down,' hissed Hunter. Dell obediently pushed his head forward until the top of his head pressed against the parcels tray. There was the smell of stale cigarette ends in the ashtray under his nose. The floor vibrated against his legs. The electric heater made a smell of singed dust. He heard the sharp, explosive noise of the bike engine, becoming suddenly louder as Hunter unwound his

171

window. A voice was asking something, and Hunter answering, 'No, I don't remember seeing anyone. Sorry.' The popping increased in loudness, then abruptly receded. 'Okay,' said Hunter, winding up the window again. 'He's gone.'

Dell hauled himself up. It wasn't clear whether he was laughing or crying. His voice was wild. He said, 'I can't stand any more of these joke crises. You should have seen us in the church this afternoon — it was too bloody farcical. It was just too bloody farcical for words. They don't even leave you any dignity any more…'

There was a clanking, and a single tank engine rumbled across the level crossing.

'For that!' said Hunter disgustedly. He raced the engine, and blared on his horn until the gates swung open. 'Where now?'

'It doesn't matter. Anywhere…'

'It matters a hell of a lot. I don't risk my life and liberty not to mention my job, just for someone to be sorry for himself. You haven't stopped running yet.'

'Okay,' said Dell. 'Turn left and then right on to the Sleaford Road.'

'I won't ask you where you want to get to.'

'I wouldn't know. Perhaps I don't want to get anywhere. I came back to Boston this morning in a diesel. It was warm and it smelled nice, and all around there was miles and miles of bugger all, but the sun was shining and once we stopped by a level crossing and there were some kids playing in the sun. The house was stone and there was washing on the line and a swing and a little dog and a pedal car. And the driver of the diesel had new overalls on and a thermos flask of tea he was drinking as we went along, and a bacon sandwich wrapped in greaseproof paper in a tin that had a picture of Windsor Castle on it. Yes, turn here.' He looked out into the darkness. 'That's one of the big dykes. The Forty Foot Drain they call it. Turn left a little way along here. It's a narrow lane, you could miss it if you're not careful.'

'You know the local topography well enough.'

'We used to go for cycle rides. Stella and I.I borrowed her old man's bike. He liked me then.'

'You were telling me about the diesel this morning.'

'Oh, it was nothing.'

'Tell me.'

'Just that … I couldn't stop wanting to cry. My eyes smarted and I wanted to — *keep* everything: the kids in the wind, and the diesel, and the driver and his tea and bacon sandwich. I wanted that journey to never end because I was so happy just to be there. I felt as if I belonged again. I knew that this was the only place to live.'

'Then you'll stay?'

Dell shook his head in the darkness. 'It's like the witch-hunt you were talking about. Once it's started there's no going back.' He added, 'Recognise where you are now? That's the main London road ahead. You turn left again to get back into the town.'

'And you?'

'You can drop me in a minute.'

Hunter stopped the car. The lights of an oncoming vehicle lit up his face but quenched the colour, so that it looked like a handsome plaster cast. He held out his hand. 'I'm sorry about everything.'

'I had it coming,' said Dell. 'Thanks for the help.'

The line of pylons was just visible against the gunmetal sky. Dell was running down the lane chopped in half like a worm, but the other way this time, with the east wind in his face bringing the brackish tang of the sea marches as well as the stink of the cabbage fields. Stella's school sprawled in darkness to his right. He ran systematically, jogging along with his elbows tucked to his sides, conserving energy as best he could. He crossed the inevitable level crossing and came to a T-junction with another lane. He stopped and exercised, drawing himself erect and throwing back his shoulders to breathe in, collapsing to breathe out, as he'd been taught in physical training in the R.A.F. He took his bearings again. The lights of town were to his left. Beyond the flat fields in front of him there seemed to be a dyke, something that made a hard edge against the sky; it was impossible to judge its direction with any accuracy, but it looked to be roughly the same as the line of pylons.

Dell bent and tied a loose shoelace, took a last breath and scouted along the new lane until he came to a five-barred gate in the hedge. He clambered over the gate and set off diagonally across the fields. On the heavy soil running was harder work. His shoes got heavier and heavier with caked mud. Once he stumbled and nearly fell. The smell of rotting vegetation became acute as he blundered through rows of dead sprouts. He jumped a water-filled ditch and found himself on fresh ploughed land. Progress was more dragging than ever. He slowed to an elephantine trot, then to walking, panting for breath. A hedge loomed up in the darkness. He fought his way through it, the branches tearing at his clothes, and stumbled on to the hard surface of a lane. He had a moment of panic — was he back on the one he'd left eight or ten minutes earlier? But the pylon line, appreciably nearer, was reassuring.

The surface made running easier again. He shambled along, only dropping to a walk to pass a lonely bungalow. The curtains were undrawn and he saw the vivid, unexpectedly blue, radiance of a television set. A man in a grey pullover was eating a solitary meal at a table, watching the screen as he ate. Dell hurried on. The lane began to bend to the left, towards the lights of the town. Dell left it again, more confidently this time, forcing himself to keep going. The smell of salt was in the air. The ploughed land gave way to muddy pasture. Dell became aware of the mute, shocked shapes of some cows. He pushed through a wire fence. The wind seemed colder suddenly. The pylons were on top of him now, leading to — and all at once he came out of a dip in the ground and it was silhouetted immediately ahead, the tall mesh fence and gallows-shapes of the transformer station. There were no lights. It was obviously unmanned. He skirted the perimeter and the ground was already sloping away. Twenty yards more and he stood on the river flood bank. From here the channel looked as if it had been gouged out of the earth. On the other side, and perhaps two hundred yards upstream, was the high wavering light and dusty white shed of the fertiliser company. The big sliding doors were open, framing two tiny figures who stood in a pool of light. And below, in the black shadow of the wharf was — yes — the *Posy*. He could see into the brightly-lit galley just below the wheelhouse and as he watched a lamp was switched on in the wheelhouse itself …

Dell ran down the bank, across the marshy grassland, nearly tripping over the skeleton ribs of a long-abandoned boat. The black water gurgled between silky banks of mud. The tide was pushing in against the flow of the river. Dell tried to estimate the force of the current. It was impossible. He closed his eyes for a moment, arming himself for what had to be done, and advanced. He trod on slippery stones, then mud was sucking at his shoes. One came off and the mud was icy-wet. He kicked off the other. A last sharp stone cut into his foot before he was alternately slithering on, and sinking into, a stretch of blacker, silkier, smoother mud. He heard bubbles soggily popping in his wake and smelt the vile smell of decay and drains and long dead fish. Suddenly the slope was getting steeper and steeper still. He struggled to keep his balance. His stockinged feet skidded wildly and next thing water was exploding all around him. He clawed himself upright, gasping and coughing and spitting out. It turned out he was still little more than knee deep. For a moment he didn't move but looked back at the bank ten yards behind him. He found he still had the box of fireworks in his hand, already going limp. He pushed it into his jacket pocket and then peeled off the jacket and let it drop into the water, and advanced again.

The icy water rose to his thighs, stabbed at his genitals, squeezed the breath from him. His foot struck something iron and hard and the pain seemed deadened and distant. He pushed himself on, leaning against the water. It clamped round his chest. Again the gradient steepened. He slithered again, threshed with his arms, recovered himself. The water was a collar round his neck and there were waves slapping into his face. He whimpered. He hadn't bargained for waves.

He kept his head back, his eyes fixed on the high shivering light as if it were a star ... he was swimming, a threshing unsynchronised breast-stroke which was all he had ever mastered. The current caught him. He tried to swim against it and waves slopped into his mouth and nose. He coughed and his hands seemed to meet no resistance; icy water was closing over him. Somehow he got his head clear again. The black shape of the *Posy* was on top of him but sliding past. He opened his mouth to shout and water filled his mouth again. Now she was only twenty feet from him, and closer inshore the tide seemed slacker.

The stern loomed above him but too high. Forward of the wheelhouse was better … only another ten feet. Dell made a last despairing floundering effort. The current was pushing him under the hull, he cried out, water drove into his mouth and nose and there was a great singing pressure in his ears. Then something hit him between the shoulder blades, a hook clawed at his clothes, a hand grabbed his wrist and bit into it like forceps as some infinitely heavy, patient weight dragged down at his legs. His chest met a hard and bruising edge, he was dimly aware of being dragged and lifted and carried and dropped. Voices sounded, near but unintelligible. He was conscious but still enclosed in a private struggle for air and life and still more air.

CHAPTER 6: SUNDAY

The *Posy* headed gamely into a heavy green sea, part riding the waves, part butting through them. The sun poured through the windows of the wheelhouse. Dell sat on the leather bench that ran the whole width of it and soaked up the greenhouse warmth. The skipper sat on a high stool like an office stool, his legs crossed, one hand on the wheel, the other reaching for a cup of coffee. On the port bow a red-lead lightship wallowed slowly nearer as the *Posy* changed course.

'Smith's Knoll, eh?' said Dell reflectively.

'Yoh, Smitt's Knoll.'

'The last of England.'

'Please?'

'Nothing.'

There was a chart on the mahogany map table. Dell had been studying it, trying to make sense of the myriad dots and numbers and hatch marks and the *Posy's* pencilled course across the bit of it that was worn faint and shiny by years of fingertips. For fifteen hours she had hugged the coast — the skyline of Yarmouth still showed if Dell poked his head out of the wheelhouse and looked back. Now at last the little ship headed east on the open sea passage that was purposely kept as short as possible.

The skipper put down his coffee cup and re-lit his pipe. He leaned across again and fiddled with the radio set in the far corner. He'd been trying to pick up Holland. He got squeaks, a snatch of distant violins and then, with sudden loudness, the cultured English tones of someone talking about music. He switched the set off.

Tony said, 'But *why* is it just stopped there all the time, why don't they drive it along?' He stood right up against the window, his little thin legs braced against the pitch of their progress. He hadn't taken his eyes off the lightship since it hove into sight.

'I told you, it's *moored* there. It's fastened to an anchor at the bottom of the sea so it stays in one place to tell other ships where they are.'

'I think it *is* going. I think perhaps it's going to London.'

'Well, you watch it carefully and tell me when I come back.' To the skipper he said, 'I'm just going below for a while.'

He squeezed past him and opened the mahogany flap and the pair of little mahogany doors and let himself down the steep companion way and through into the cabin where he'd first met the skipper. Nancy had been washing clothes and nappies. She had them hung out on a piece of wire she'd stretched across from bulkhead to stovepipe.

Dell said, 'How's the baby?'

'She's *asleep* again. It must be the rocking that does it. Mind you, she didn't get much last night.'

'Tell me about it, about last night.'

'I've told you.'

'Tell me about it again. All I remember is being heaved aboard and then carried somewhere and then lying in this little tiny cabin at the rear, wrapped in a blanket, on a bunk that smelled of old bacon, something like that, and the cook — was it the cook? — telling me to keep quiet... Go on, tell.'

She sighed and laughed and said, '*Well...*' Her face was glowing from the sea air and the exertions of washing. She was wearing the old white sweater he'd given her, it had a polo neck, and a tweed skirt; her legs were bare. 'Well I couldn't see much, but I poked my head out whenever I got the chance.

179

First we went along a channel to the sea and it was funny, like driving along a road, almost; I mean it was dark and sort of eerie, but it was ever so narrow and you could see things on land very close, like a house or a little church once. Then it started to get wide and the boat began to sway about and we were in the sea —'

'The Wash.'

'All right, the Wash. Where King John lost his laundry, they used to tell us. And you could see the lights of towns. Skegness, the cook said one of them was, where there's a Butlins. And then there was this searchlight shining across the water out of the dark. I wasn't supposed to be watching. I thought for certain it was all up with us. But it was only the pilot being taken off. And d'you know? — he was just an ordinary little fellow in a blue mac, as if he'd come to read the meters, but he went and hung out over the side of the ship and hopped across to this other boat like nobodies business. I can tell you, I wouldn't have done it for — for anything.'

Dell sat on the bed. It wasn't a bunk, it really was more like a proper bed. 'Come here.' He patted the cover beside him.

She looked at him with grey eyes that were grave again. 'Where are we going? I mean, it's not just Holland, is it? That's only the start. Where are we going to finish? Will there be somewhere proper for —'

'Look, leave it, will you? I don't want to think about it. Not yet, anyway. We got out, didn't we? We're on this ship. For the moment we're safe.' He said more softly, 'We're cut off. No one can get at us. Let's make the most of it.'

She came and stood in front of him. He ran his hand up the back of her leg. It was solid and cool. 'Hallo, hallo. Who's not wearing any knicks?'

'I washed them.'

'Go on. You fancy the captain.'

'Oh, you!' She gave him a playful punch. 'Hey, leave off. What if someone came in?'

'No one's got any business to come in.' The skirt unbuttoned at the side.

'They'd get an eyeful if they did, at the moment.'

'I like you in that old white pullover.'

'It's shrunk.'

'That's why I like you in it.'

She murmured, 'You shouldn't do that to me.'

He drew her down.

'Come on, love.'

When it was over Nancy seemed to draw away from him.

She turned her head. Her body began to shake. She was sobbing with very deep sobs and the tears ran down from her eyes straight on to the pillow. 'What's going to become of Tony?' she whispered. 'What will he do? Will it ever come all right for him, wherever we go?'

A NOTE TO THE READER

If you have enjoyed this novel enough to leave a review on **Amazon** and **Goodreads**, then we would be truly grateful.
Sapere Books

Sapere Books is an exciting new publisher of brilliant fiction and popular history.

To find out more about our latest releases and our monthly bargain books visit our website: **saperebooks.com**

Printed in Great Britain
by Amazon